entertainment

culture

animals

核心 素養
108課綱

In Focus
英語閱讀
活用五大關鍵技巧

1

作者 | Owain Mckimm / Shara Dupuis / Laura Phelps
譯者 | 劉嘉珮
審訂 | Richard Luhrs

MP3

寂天雲 APP

如何下載 MP3 音檔

❶ 寂天雲 APP 聆聽：掃描書上 QR Code 下載
「寂天雲－英日語學習隨身聽」APP。加入會員
後，用 APP 內建掃描器再次掃描書上 QR
Code，即可使用 APP 聆聽音檔。

❷ 官網下載音檔：請上「寂天閱讀網」
（www.icosmos.com.tw），註冊會員／登入後，
搜尋本書，進入本書頁面，點選「MP3 下載」
下載音檔，存於電腦等其他播放器聆聽使用。

U0033944

Contents Chart 目錄

Introduction 簡介

　　本套書依程度共分四冊，專為初中級讀者編寫。每冊包含50篇閱讀文章、30餘種文體與題材。各冊分級主要針對文章字數多寡、字級難易度、文法深淺、句子長度來區分。生活化的主題配合多元化的體裁，讓讀者透過教材，體驗豐富多樣的語言學習經驗，提昇學習興趣，增進學習效果。

字數 （每篇）	國中 1200 單字（每篇）	國中 1201- 2000 單字 （每篇）	高中 7000 (3, 4, 5 級) （每篇）	文法程度	句子長度
Book 1 120–150	93%	7 字	3 字	（國一） first year	15 字
Book 2 150–180	86%	15 字	6 字	（國二） second year	18 字
Book 3 180–210	82%	30 字	7 字	（國三） third year	25 字
Book 4 210–250	75%	50 字	12 字	（國三進階） advanced	28 字

本書架構
閱讀文章

　　本套書涵蓋豐富且多元的主題與體裁。文章形式廣泛蒐羅各類生活中常見的實用體裁，包含短文、詩、對話、廣告、部落格、行事曆、宣傳手冊、雜誌文章、新聞短片等三十餘種，以日常相關的生活經驗為重點編寫設計，幫助加強基礎閱讀能力，提升基本英語溝通能力，為基礎生活英語紮根。

　　收錄大量題材有趣、多元且生活化的短文，範圍囊括青少年生活、家庭、教育、娛樂、健康、節慶、動物、藝術、文學、科學、文化、旅遊等三十餘種，主題多元化且貼近生活經驗，可激起學生學習興趣，協助學生理解不同領域知識。

閱讀測驗

每篇短文後,皆接有五題閱讀理解選擇題,評量學生對文章的理解程度。閱讀測驗所訓練學生的閱讀技巧包括:

文章中心思想
(Main Idea)/
主題(Subject Matter)

支持性細節
(Supporting Details)

從上下文猜測字義
(Words in Context)

文意推論
(Making Inferences)

看懂影像圖表
(Visualizing
Comprehension)

文章中心思想(Main Idea)

閱讀文章時,讀者可以試著問自己:「**作者想要傳達什麼訊息?**」透過審視理解的方式,檢視自己是否了解文章意義。

文章主題(Subject Matter)

這類問題幫助讀者專注在所閱讀的文章中,在閱讀文章前幾行後,讀者應該問自己:「**這篇文章是關於什麼?**」這麼做能幫助你立刻集中注意力,快速理解文章內容,進而掌握整篇文章脈絡。

支持性細節（Supporting Details）

每篇文章都是由細節組成來支持主題句。「**支持性細節**」包括範例、說明、敘述、定義、比較、對比和比喻。

從上下文猜測字義（Words in Context）

由上下文猜生字意義，是英文閱讀中一項很重要的策略。弄錯關鍵字詞的意思會導致誤解作者想要傳達的觀點。

文意推論（Making Inferences）

推論性的問題會要讀者歸納文章中已有的資訊，來思考、推理，並且將線索連結起來，推論可能的事實，這種問題的目的是訓練讀者的批判性思考和邏輯性。

看懂影像圖表（Visualizing Comprehension）

這類問題考驗讀者理解視覺資料的能力，包括表格、圖片、地圖等，或是索引、字典，學會運用這些圖像資料能增進你對文章的整體理解。

How Do I Use This Book? 使用導覽

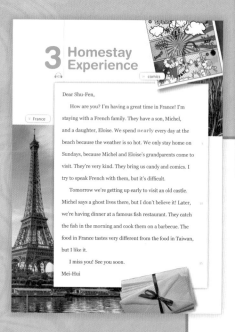

主題多元化

題材有趣且多元，貼近日常生活經驗，包含青少年生活、教育、娛樂、科學、藝術與文學等，激發學生學習興趣，協助學生理解不同領域知識。

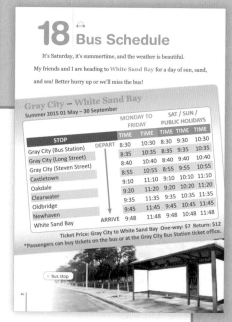

體裁多樣化

廣納生活中常見的實用體裁，包含短文、詩、對話、廣告、部落格、行事曆等，以日常相關生活經驗設計編寫，為基礎生活英語紮根。

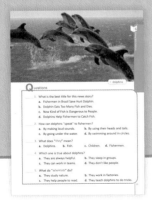

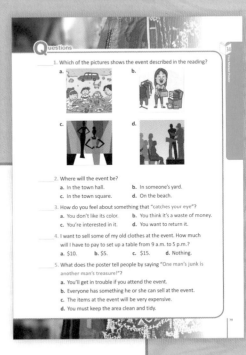

閱讀技巧練習題

左頁文章、右頁測驗的設計方式，短文後皆接有五題閱讀理解選擇題，評量學生對文章的理解程度，訓練五大閱讀技巧。

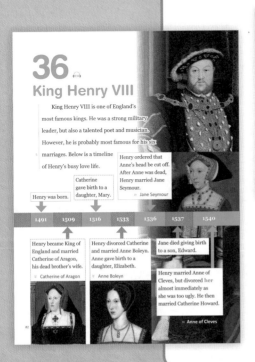

豐富多彩的圖表

運用大量彩色圖表與圖解，搭配文章輕鬆學習，以視覺輔助記憶，學習成效加倍。

1 The Power of a Smile

Are you smiling right now? What makes you smile? Maybe you smile when you see your friends, eat chocolate cake, or win a prize. Doctors think we should smile often, because it's good for our bodies and minds. When you

5 smile:

• you feel happy,

• you make others feel happy,

• you look more beautiful, and

• you can "speak" without language!

10 Smiling means the same thing in every country in the world. There is even a "Smile Power Day" on June 15, when people smile at strangers. But be careful! Most people will

⌃ prize

⌄ smile

notice the difference between a real smile and a **fake** one. When your smile is real, you use your mouth and your eyes. When your smile isn't real, you only use your mouth.

15

Why don't you try **it**? Smile for real at your teacher; does he or she smile at you, too?

⌃ fake smile

Questions

_____ 1. What can we learn from the reading?
    a. Doctors shouldn't smile.   **b.** Teachers often smile.
    c. Smiling is good for you.   **d.** Don't smile at strangers.

_____ 2. Which of the following is not true?
    a. "Smile Power Day" is on June 15.
    b. "Smile Power Day" is on July 15.
    c. Smiling makes you look beautiful.
    d. Smiling makes you feel happy.

_____ 3. What does "fake" mean?
    a. Happy.   **b.** Beautiful.   **c.** False.   **d.** Comfortable.

_____ 4. How do you know when someone is happy?
    a. She smiles with all of her face.
    b. She only smiles with her mouth.
    c. She spends time with her friends.
    d. She eats a lot of chocolate cake.

_____ 5. What does "it" mean?
    a. Winning.   **b.** Talking.   **c.** Learning.   **d.** Smiling.

2 Mother's Day Card

To the World's Greatest Mom,

You're the kindest, most caring,
most wonderful mother I could ever wish for.
Thank you for always taking care of me.
Thank you for always cheering me up when I feel sad.
And thank you for keeping me out of trouble!

I want you to know that you're not just my mom;
you're also my best friend. So I'm sending you lots and
lots of love and kisses on this special day.

And, I told Dad to stop being so lazy and to give you
the day off, and he said he would. So if he's not helping
out around the house, he's breaking his promise
(I hope he gave you breakfast in bed; I did remind him).

All my love,

Your loving daughter,

Jane

P.S. I hope you liked the flowers.
    I know tulips are your favorite!

Questions

_____ 1. If this were a card, what would it look like?

a.

b.

c.

d.

_____ 2. What do we know from the reading?

   a. Jane has children of her own.

   b. Jane's father made her mother breakfast in bed.

   c. Jane does not get along well with her father.

   d. Jane and her mother have a good relationship.

_____ 3. What are "**tulips**"?

   a. A type of card   b. A type of food.

   c. A type of flower.   d. A type of song.

_____ 4. What did Jane mean when she told her father to give her mother "**the day off**"?

   a. He should take her mother out for a meal.

   b. He should do the housework for her mother.

   c. He should help her mother call in sick for work.

   d. He should watch TV with her mother.

_____ 5. What does "**cheer someone up**" most likely mean?

   a. Correct someone's mistake.

   b. Give someone money.

   c. Laugh at someone.

   d. Make someone feel happy.

3 Homestay Experience

» comics

» France

Dear Shu-Fen,

How are you? I'm having a great time in France! I'm staying with a French family. They have a son, Michael, and a daughter, Eloise. We spend **nearly** every day at the beach because the weather is so hot. We only stay home on 5
Sundays because Michael and Eloise's grandparents come to visit. They're very kind. They bring us candy and comics. I try to speak French with them, but it's difficult.

Tomorrow we're getting up early to visit an old castle. Michael says a ghost lives there, but I don't believe it! Later, 10
we're having dinner at a famous fish restaurant. They catch the fish in the morning and cook them on a barbecue. The food in France tastes very different from the food in Taiwan, but I like it.

I miss you! See you soon. 15

Mei-Hui

⌃ barbecue

 uestions

____ 1. What should Mei-Hui's postcard look like?

a.    b.    c.    d.

____ 2. Where is Mei-Hui going tomorrow morning?
    a. To a castle.   **b.** To a store.   **c.** To school.   **d.** To a restaurant.

____ 3. What does "**nearly**" mean?
    a. Also.   **b.** Never.   **c.** Almost.   **d.** Slowly.

____ 4. Which sentence is true?
    a. Mei-Hui doesn't enjoy French food.
    b. Mei-Hui doesn't think she'll see a ghost.
    c. Mei-Hui can speak French very well.
    d. Mei-Hui goes to the beach on Sundays.

____ 5. Why does Mei-Hui like Michael and Eloise's grandparents?
    a. The grandparents give them gifts.
    b. The grandparents cook for them.
    c. The grandparents tell them stories.
    d. The grandparents take them to the park.

4

^ headache

^ screen

Too Much Screen Time Is Bad for Your Eyes!

Doctor: Hello. How can I help?

Man: I'm getting a lot of headaches, but I don't know why.

Doctor: How is your **diet**?

Man: I only eat healthy food! That's not the problem.

5 Doctor: Okay. Can I check your eyes? They're very dry and red.

  How often do you use a computer?

Man: Every day. I work in an office.

Doctor: And what do you usually do after work?

Man: I chat with friends on my phone, or I watch a movie.

10 Doctor: So you use a computer all day, and then you look at

  more screens in the evening! **Of course you're getting**

  headaches!

Man: What can I do? I can't live without the Internet!

Doctor: First, make sure your screens are not too bright. Second,

15 take a break every 20 minutes. And last, try to find a hobby

  outside! That will be good for your general health, too.

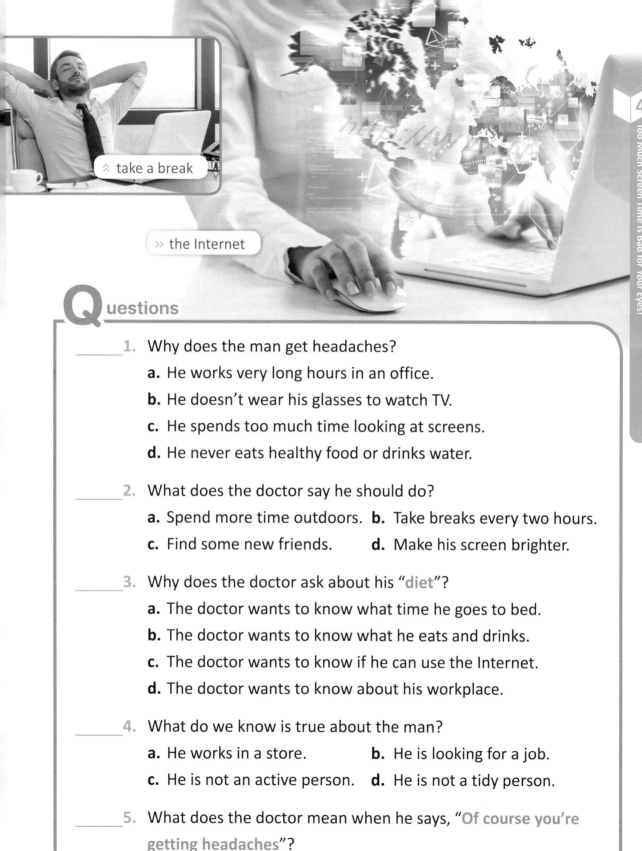

take a break

» the Internet

Questions

_____ 1. Why does the man get headaches?

a. He works very long hours in an office.

b. He doesn't wear his glasses to watch TV.

c. He spends too much time looking at screens.

d. He never eats healthy food or drinks water.

_____ 2. What does the doctor say he should do?

a. Spend more time outdoors.   **b.** Take breaks every two hours.

c. Find some new friends.   **d.** Make his screen brighter.

_____ 3. Why does the doctor ask about his "**diet**"?

a. The doctor wants to know what time he goes to bed.

b. The doctor wants to know what he eats and drinks.

c. The doctor wants to know if he can use the Internet.

d. The doctor wants to know about his workplace.

_____ 4. What do we know is true about the man?

a. He works in a store.   **b.** He is looking for a job.

c. He is not an active person. **d.** He is not a tidy person.

_____ 5. What does the doctor mean when he says, "**Of course you're getting headaches**"?

a. The doctor is not surprised. **b.** The doctor wants to leave.

c. The doctor feels unhappy.   **d.** The doctor has a headache.

5 Saying Sorry to a Friend

> go shopping

ice cream

> department store

To: tina_134@funmail.com

From: jenny1435@pcmailbox.com

Date: Sat, Jun 7, 2014 at 9:00 p.m.

Subject: I'm sorry :(

Tina,

I'm so sorry about what happened. Amy invited me to go shopping with her, and I said yes. I know you hate her after she said all those mean things about you in school.

I just didn't think. You are my best friend, and I promise never to speak to her again. **I didn't even have a good time.** All she did the whole time was talk about herself. It was SO boring!

Can I at least do something to make it up to you? How about going out for ice cream tomorrow, to that place you really like in the department store? And I'm buying. I really feel bad about this, Tina. I hope you can forgive me.

Your friend always,

Jenny

Questions

_____ 1. What is Jenny's main reason for writing this email?

    a. To ask Tina to forgive her.   **b.** To invite Tina to hang out.

    c. To complain about Amy.   **d.** To tell Tina about her day.

_____ 2. Tina writes "How about going out for ice cream tomorrow?" What day is tomorrow?

    a. Monday.   **b.** Saturday.   **c.** Sunday.   **d.** Friday.

_____ 3. What does Jenny mean when she writes "I didn't even have a good time"?

    a. She didn't listen.   **b.** She didn't have fun.

    c. She arrived late.   **d.** She forgot what they did.

_____ 4. What is most likely true about Tina, Jenny, and Amy?

    a. They're classmates.   **b.** They're cousins.

    c. They work together.   **d.** They go to the same church.

_____ 5. Tina forgives Jenny and they go out the next day. They take a picture together. Which is most likely the picture?

    a.   **b.**   **c.**   **d.**

6 Fishing With Dolphins

>> net

Dolphins in Laguna, south Brazil, are helping fishermen with their work. As they swim, the dolphins push groups of fish near the fishermen. When the group is big enough, the dolphins make a sign with their heads or tails. This way, the fishermen know when to throw their nets. 5

This shows that dolphins can work together, and work with people. It also shows that dolphins are intelligent because **they** learned to do it by themselves. Dolphins understand that by helping 10 the fishermen, they also get more fish to eat.

Scientists studied the dolphins in Brazil for two years. They are interested in this story because not every dolphin wants to help. This means that dolphins are like people: some are helpful, and 15 some are not.

⌃ fisherman

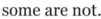

>> tail

22

⌃ dolphins

Questions

_____ 1. What is the best title for this news story?

    a. Fishermen in Brazil Save Hurt Dolphin.

    b. Dolphin Eats Too Many Fish and Dies.

    c. New Kind of Fish Is Dangerous to People.

    d. Dolphins Help Fishermen to Catch Fish.

_____ 2. How can dolphins "speak" to fishermen?

    a. By making loud sounds.   **b.** By using their heads and tails.

    c. By going under the water.   **d.** By swimming around in circles.

_____ 3. What does "they" mean?

    a. Dolphins.   **b.** Fish.   **c.** Children.   **d.** Fishermen.

_____ 4. Which one is true about dolphins?

    a. They are always helpful.   **b.** They sleep in groups.

    c. They can work in teams.   **d.** They don't like people.

_____ 5. What do "scientists" do?

    a. They study nature.   **b.** They work in factories.

    c. They help people to read.   **d.** They teach dolphins to do tricks.

7 Teens' Emotional Health

⌃ teenagers

Welcome to this book, *How Are You Feeling*?
We know it's not easy being a teenager. Your
teachers give you too much homework, and your
parents don't give you enough freedom! Sometimes you

5 have problems with friends, brothers, and sisters. **One
day** you feel happy and excited, **and the next** sad or
angry.

You're not a child anymore. Your mind and body are
growing fast, and that can be hard to understand. The

10 good news is, this happens to everyone, so you're not
alone.

This book will help you to understand some difficult
parts of teenage life. In the first part of the book, we
will explain why your feelings change quickly. In the

15 second, we will give you some ideas about how to feel
better! We hope you enjoy reading it.

« freedom

Questions

_____ 1. What is the reading mainly trying to say?

   a. Teenagers should fight for their freedom.

   b. It's important to be nice to people.

   c. Students should read more books.

   d. It's okay to have all sorts of feelings.

_____ 2. Which source of teen problems is not mentioned in the reading?

   a. Family.   **b.** Friends.   **c.** Money.   **d.** School.

_____ 3. What does "alone" mean?

   a. Very angry.   **b.** Late for class.

   c. Too young.   **d.** With nobody.

_____ 4. What does the writer say about teenagers?

   a. Adults can make their lives more difficult.

   b. They should stop fighting with their parents.

   c. If they don't enjoy reading, it doesn't matter.

   d. They are always happy and excited after school.

_____ 5. What does "One day . . ., and the next . . ." show?

   a. That teenagers sleep a lot.

   b. That feelings change fast.

   c. That school life is interesting.

   d. That friends are important.

8 Clean the Neighborhood

⌃ garbage

Mike: Look at **that**! Someone threw their

garbage right there on the sidewalk.

Bill: I know. This neighborhood is becoming such a mess.

Mike: We should do something about it. We need to get people

5   to care more about the state of the neighborhood.

Bill: Good idea. Let's call a neighborhood meeting.

That way we can talk to everyone at once.

Mike: Right, but what if people don't listen to us?

Bill: We need something to catch their attention. I know!

10   Why don't we take photos of all the trash we see on the

ground over the next few days? Then we can show all the

pictures at the meeting.

Mike: Good idea. That way everyone can see for themselves how

big the problem is.

15 Bill: Yeah. Maybe we can even get a group together to help clean

the place up.

Mike: Great! Okay, let's start by inviting everyone to the meeting . . .

>> neighborhood

 sidewalk

Questions

_____ 1. What are Bill and Mike talking about?
   a. Meeting their new neighbors.
   b. Getting together with friends.
   c. Keeping their area free of garbage.
   d. How to take good photos.

_____ 2. What are the two going to use to
   catch people's attention at their meeting?
   a. Shocking pictures.   b. A funny song.
   c. A famous speaker.   d. Colorful clothes.

_____ 3. What could "**that**" mean in the reading?
   a. Bill's house.   b. Mike's phone.
   c. A water bottle.   d. A set of car keys.

_____ 4. What do you think Bill and Mike will talk about next?
   a. What they should wear to the meeting.
   b. Who should speak at the meeting.
   c. A good date and time for the meeting.
   d. What snacks they should bring to the meeting.

_____ 5. After the meeting, Bill, Mike, and a few other people
   formed a group. Which of these is a picture of that group?

   a.   **b.**   **c.**   **d.**

9 Homesick Blues

I woke up this morning,

With a strange pain in my chest.

I woke up this morning,

With a strange pain in my chest.

5 I thought, "Maybe I've got the flu or something."

So I lay down and took a rest. I slept for a few hours,

But the pain still wouldn't go. Oh, I rested and I rested,

But the pain still wouldn't go. I even took some medicine,

But the pain was worse than before.

10 I went to the doctor; he said, "Boy, *let me take a look at you*."

I went to the doctor; he said, "Boy, what you've got is not the flu.

When's the last time you saw your mother?

You've got the homesick blues."

He said, "What you need is your mother's cooking,

15 Then you'll feel *right as rain*."

He said, "Your old ma's love is what you're needing;

Then you'll be just fine again."

So I'm going home to see my mother;

She's going to take my homesick blues away.

Questions

_____ 1. What is the writer trying to say?

    a. He's seriously ill.

    b. His parents are angry with him.

    c. He misses his mother.

    d. He has no home.

_____ 2. What does the writer first think causes the pain in his chest?

    a. A sickness.   **b.** Being tired.

    c. A broken heart.   **d.** Smoking too much.

_____ 3. How do you feel if you are "**right as rain**"?

    a. Sad.   **b.** A little nervous.

    c. Homesick.   **d.** Just fine.

_____ 4. What does the doctor think the writer should do?

    a. Cook a meal for his mother.

    b. Call his mother on the phone.

    c. Visit his mother.

    d. Buy his mother a gift.

_____ 5. What does the doctor mean when he says, "**Let me take a look at you**"?

    a. "I don't know what's wrong with you."

    b. "My eyes are bad; come closer."

    c. "Allow me to examine you."

    d. "Stop covering your face."

10 How to Make a Jack-O'-Lantern

010

Dad: Okay, let's begin.

Jenny: What do we do first?

Dad: First, take this bread knife, and carefully cut out a lid on the top of the pumpkin.

5 Jenny: Like this?

Dad: Yes, good.

Jenny: Now what?

Dad: Now we scoop out the insides with the spoon.

10 Jenny: Can I use my hands?

Dad: Ha, ha. Sure, if you like.

» spoon

^ pumpkins

^ jack-o'-lantern

Questions

_____ 1. What is Jenny's father teaching her?
- **a.** How to operate something.
- **b.** How to make something.
- **c.** How to cook something.
- **d.** How to take care of something.

_____ 2. Which of the following do they not use?
- **a.** A spoon. **b.** A knife. **c.** A fork. **d.** A pen.

_____ 3. What does "**tricky**" mean in the reading?
- **a.** Difficult. **b.** Safe. **c.** Easy. **d.** Impossible.

Jenny: Are we going to throw the insides away?

Dad: No. That would be wasteful. We'll give the
        pumpkin meat to Mom. She can use it to
15   make pumpkin pie later!

Jenny: Now what?

Dad: Now, draw a scary face on the pumpkin with
        this pen. Next, we cut out the face with the
        knife. This can be **tricky**, so I'll do this part.

20 Jenny: Now we just have to put in the candle, right?

Dad: That's right. And there you have it—a scary
        jack-o'-lantern!

 candle

_____ 4. Which of the following is Jenny and her father's jack-o'-lantern?

a.    b.    c.    d.

_____ 5. What will Jenny and her family most likely have for dessert later?

   a. Ice cream.   **b.** Cake.   **c.** Pie.   **d.** Pudding.

11 Finding a Roommate

NOTICE 1:

Do you need a roommate?

I'm Tara from Australia. I'm 19 and I study history. I am very clean, tidy and friendly! I want to live with someone who likes animals and movies. I am learning to play the cello, so sometimes I practice in the evening.

If you don't mind the noise, call me on 089-435-7139 or email tarakeenan@knights.edu.au.

Questions

_____ 1. Why do Tara and Helen write these notices?
   a. They need someone to teach them English.
   b. They need someone to share a room with.
   c. They need someone to look after their pets.
   d. They need someone to play in their bands.

_____ 2. Where does Helen come from?
   a. Australia.   b. England.   c. The United States.   d. Canada.

_____ 3. What is a "cello"?
   a. A game.   b. A person.   c. An instrument.   d. An animal.

« roommate

« draw

NOTICE 2:

I need a roommate!

My name is Helen, and I'm from the United States. I'm looking for a girl between 18 and 20 years old who can speak English. I want someone quiet, who will keep the room tidy. I love cats and dogs, drawing and playing baseball. I get up very early. If that's okay with you, why don't we share a room? Give me a call at 089-237-2894 or email htyo@gmail.com.

» messy

« tidy

____ **4.** What do Tara and Helen both think is important?

     a. To be clean.   **b.** To be early.   **c.** To be friendly.   **d.** To be quiet.

____ **5.** Which sentence is true?

     a. Tara likes pets, but Helen doesn't.

     b. Helen likes pets, but Tara doesn't.

     c. Both Tara and Helen like pets.

     d. Neither Tara nor Helen likes pets.

12 Don't Eat Too Fast

» rush food

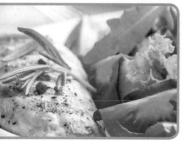

⌃ meal

⌃ taste

Man:	Shall we go to that new restaurant tonight?
Woman:	It's no fun going to a restaurant with you. You always eat so fast!
Man:	So? I enjoy eating.
Woman:	I enjoy it, too! That's why I take my time. How can you taste your food properly when you finish in 10 minutes?
Man:	If you wait too long, the food gets cold.
Woman:	But don't you get a stomachache?
Man:	No, I don't.
Woman:	**In my opinion,** meals should be a pleasure. It's nice to eat slowly and talk at the same time.
Man:	We can talk before and after the meal. I don't understand you at all. Do you want to have dinner with me tonight or not?
Woman:	Oh, I'll come with you—if you promise not to **rush** your food for once!

5

10

15

« stomachache

Questions

____ 1. What does the woman think?
   a. You shouldn't go to restaurants every night.
   b. You shouldn't speak while you're eating.
   c. You should teach your children how to cook.
   d. You should eat slowly and enjoy your food.

____ 2. Why does the man eat his food quickly?
   a. He wants to eat while it's hot.   **b.** He has to go back to work.
   c. He always feels hungry.   **d.** He finds mealtimes boring.

____ 3. Why does the woman say "In my opinion" in the reading?
   a. She agrees with the man.
   b. She is saying her idea, not a fact.
   c. She doesn't understand something.
   d. She wants to give an example.

____ 4. Which one is true?
   a. The man always gets a stomachache after eating.
   b. The woman and the man will eat together tonight.
   c. The woman always finishes her food in 10 minutes.
   d. The man enjoys eating, but not the woman.

____ 5. What does "rush" mean?
   a. Prepare.   **b.** Hurry.   **c.** Wait.   **d.** Know.

13

Homer, the Blind Wonder Cat

Posted: 22 August, 2013 4:12 p.m.

Goodbye, Homer

Everyone who reads this blog knows how much I love cats! I'm feeling sad today because **one** of the world's most famous cats has died. Homer, the "blind
5 wonder cat," was 11 years old.

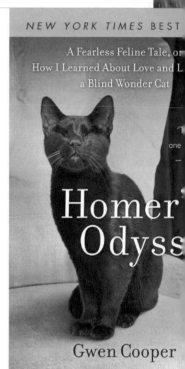

NEW YORK TIMES BEST

A Fearless Feline Tale, or How I Learned About Love and L a Blind Wonder Cat

Homer' Odyss

Gwen Cooper

⌃ Gwen wrote a book about Homer.

Homer's owner, Gwen Cooper, wrote about him on the Internet. People in many countries wanted to read about him. Gwen told stories about how Homer was
10 very brave although he couldn't see. One night, when a man broke into Gwen's house, Homer attacked him and saved Gwen. In 2009, she wrote a book about Homer which raised money for other animals.

Because of Homer, people changed their ideas about blind
15 cats. Before, if a kitten was born blind, doctors didn't save it. But now, they understand that blind animals can have good lives.

Goodbye, Homer, and thank you. **Rest in peace**.

Questions

_____ 1. What is the reading about?

    a. A writer with lots of cats.

    b. A doctor who saved a cat.

    c. A famous cat that died.

    d. A book about blind animals.

_____ 2. Which one is not true?

    a. Gwen Cooper wrote a book.

    b. Homer the cat couldn't see.

    c. Gwen Cooper is 11 years old.

    d. Homer the cat was brave.

_____ 3. What does "**one**" mean in the reading?

    a. A cat.   **b.** A blind person.

    c. A bad man.   **d.** A short story.

_____ 4. What do we know about Homer?

    a. He learned to use the Internet.

    b. He cost Gwen a lot of money.

    c. He felt sad when Gwen felt sad.

    d. He was popular all over the world.

_____ 5. Why do people say "**rest in peace**"?

    a. They feel happy that someone was born.

    b. They feel sad that someone died.

    c. They want someone to be quiet.

    d. They want someone to go to sleep.

 attack

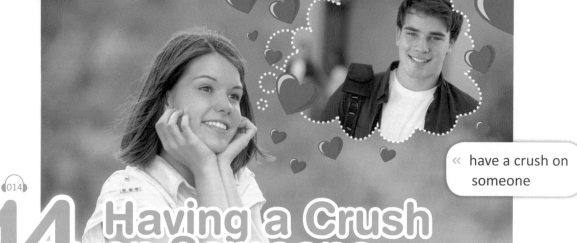

« have a crush on someone

14 Having a Crush on Someone

Jenny

Kate

J So, did you talk to Chris about me?

K Yeah. I did.

J Oh, my God; I'm so nervous! What did he say? Did he say he likes me?

K Well, yeah, he said he likes you . . .

J What? Really? Oh, my God! I'm so happy!

K Wait, Jenny. Before you get too excited, he said he likes you, but not in that way.

J Wait . . . What? What does that mean?

K It means he likes you as a friend, but nothing more. I'm sorry. I know how crazy you are about him. I guess he just doesn't feel the same way.

J Okay. But wait. What were his exact words?

K I asked him, "Do you have a girlfriend?" and he said no. And then I said, "What about Jenny?" and he said, "I think she's a nice person, but **she's not really my type**."

⌃ heartbroken

>> girlfriend

Questions

_____ 1. What's the main topic of the conversation?

    a. What kind of girl Chris likes.

    b. What Chris thinks about Jenny.

    c. Whether Chris has a girlfriend or not.

    d. How much Jenny likes Chris.

_____ 2. What do we know about Chris?

    a. He likes Kate.   **b.** He thinks Jenny is dull.

    c. He's single.   **d.** He's in Jenny's class.

_____ 3. What does the phrase "**she's not really my type**" mean?

    a. Jenny is not a very nice person.

    b. Jenny doesn't know how to use a computer.

    c. Jenny's not the kind of girl Chris usually likes.

    d. Jenny and Chris are interested in the same things.

_____ 4. Why does Jenny ask Kate what Chris's exact words were?

    a. She's thinks maybe Kate got the wrong idea.

    b. She thinks that Chris likes Kate, not her.

    c. She doesn't understand Kate's English.

    d. She wants to tell her mother what Chris said.

_____ 5. In instant messages, people often show their feelings by sending pictures of faces. Which face do you think Jenny will send Kate in her next message?

    a.   **b.**   **c.**   **d.**

15 Music Radio

♪ *Oh, the music has me smiling.*
It's the best best medicine . . . ♪

"The Best Medicine" there by Adrian Williams. Great song. That was for Mike in Newbridge.

5   Welcome, if you just **tuned in**, to the Breakfast Show with me, Christian O'Brian. Today we're playing the songs that you choose, so text us with your favorite song at 877-543 and I'll do my very best to play it for you before the end of the show.

10   Coming up a little later we'll have "Time's Up" by the Mega Sisters, and after that "Leave Me Be" by Simon and the Twins. But next up we have "Party All Night" by the Friday Girls. This song is for Pat in Oakdale. Hope you enjoy the song, Pat. The Friday Girls with

15   "Party All Night."

♪ *It's Friday night. Oh yeah!*
It's Friday night. Oh yeah! . . .♪

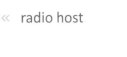
« radio host

⌃ text

⌃ tune in

Questions

1. What is special about today's show?
   a. There's music by Adrian Williams.
   b. The listeners choose the songs.
   c. Christian O'Brian is the DJ.
   d. It's on the radio.

2. Who sings the song "Party All Night"?
   a. Adrian Williams.   b. The Mega Sisters.
   c. Simon and the Twins.   d. The Friday Girls.

3. What do you do if you "**tune in**" to a radio show?
   a. You turn it off.   b. You turn the sound up.
   c. You start to listen to it. d. You call the DJ.

4. When does the show air?
   a. In the morning.   b. In the afternoon.
   c. In the evening.   d. Late at night.

5. What is Mike in Newbridge's favorite song?
   a. "Leave Me Be."   b. "Time's Up."
   c. "The Best Medicine."   d. "Party All Night."

16 Songkran

People use water with flowers in it to wash the Buddha statues.

Throwing water brings good luck for the next year.

In my country, Thailand, our most important festival is Songkran. It's our New Year festival. It always happens in April, and it's always a lot of fun. Everyone knows about this festival because you can throw water on other people! **This** brings good luck for the next year. You can buy delicious food on the street, like papaya or chicken with special sauce.

Many people go back to their hometowns during Songkran. They want to spend time with their families. On the first day, they clean their houses. On the second

Songkran festival in Thailand

day, they play games with water.
On the third day, they visit the
temple and wash the Buddha
statues. They use water with
15 flowers in it, so the statues smell
nice and fresh. Songkran is
everyone's favorite time of the year.

Questions

_____ 1. What is the reading about?

    a. A vacation.   **b.** Thai food.   **c.** Families.   **d.** A festival.

_____ 2. What do people do on the third day of Songkran?

    a. Drink papaya juice.   **b.** Go to the temple.

    c. Play water games.   **d.** Clean their houses.

_____ 3. What does the word "**This**" mean?

    a. Throwing water.   **b.** Dancing outside.

    c. Cooking chicken.   **d.** Visiting family.

_____ 4. How does the writer feel during Songkran?

    a. Happy.   **b.** Tired.   **c.** Sad.   **d.** Bored.

_____ 5. What do we know from the reading?

    a. People in Thailand think Songkran is boring.

    b. People in Thailand love Songkran.

    c. People in Thailand eat at restaurants on Songkran.

    d. People in Thailand build statues on Songkran.

>> hide

17 An Awkward Moment

017

⌃ partner

⌃ friendly

It was Diane's first day at her new school. She was worried no one would like her. Her first class of the day was English. The teacher, Mr. Smith, asked the students to work with a partner to complete a project. All the students

5 in the class quickly found someone to work with, except for Diane. So, Mr. Smith offered to work with her. A few of her classmates laughed. Diane wanted to hide.

At lunch, a friendly girl named Anne asked Diane to eat with her and her friends. She asked Diane how her

10 first day of school was going. Diane replied, "Okay, but I don't like my English teacher. He made me be his partner. He's so strange!"

The entire table became **silent**. Diane didn't know what she had said wrong. Finally, Anne's friend Tina said,

15 "Mr. Smith is Anne's father." Diane felt like she was going to die.

Questions

_____ 1. What is this story mainly about?

a. Diane making a fool of herself.

b. Anne inviting Diane to her house.

c. Diane getting along with everyone at school.

d. Diane's English teacher being mean to her.

_____ 2. Why did Diane want to hide in English class?

a. She didn't know how to complete the work.

b. She was late for class.

c. She had to be partners with the teacher.

d. She didn't make any friends.

_____ 3. What is it like when the whole table is "silent"?

a. Everyone is laughing.   b. Everyone is studying.

c. No one is talking.   d. No one is listening.

_____ 4. Why was Diane worried about going to school?

a. She didn't study for the test.   b. She was going to be late.

c. She didn't want to get lost.   d. She was new to the school.

_____ 5. Why did Diane feel like she was going to die?

a. She didn't do well on her English homework.

b. She said something unkind about Anne's father.

c. She didn't want to eat lunch with Tina.

d. She ate something bad for lunch.

18 | Bus Schedule

🎧 018

It's Saturday, it's summertime, and the weather is beautiful.

My friends and I are heading to **White Sand Bay** for a day of sun, sand, and sea! Better hurry up or we'll miss the bus!

Gray City — White Sand Bay
Summer 2015 01 May – 30 September

STOP	MONDAY TO FRIDAY		SAT / SUN / PUBLIC HOLIDAYS		
	TIME	TIME	TIME	TIME	TIME
Gray City (Bus Station) — DEPART	8:30	10:30	8:30	9:30	10:30
Gray City (Long Street)	8:35	10:35	8:35	9:35	10:35
Gray City (Steven Street)	8:40	10:40	8:40	9:40	10:40
Castletown	8:55	10:55	8:55	9:55	10:55
Oakdale	9:10	11:10	9:10	10:10	11:10
Clearwater	9:20	11:20	9:20	10:20	11:20
Oldbridge	9:35	11:35	9:35	10:35	11:35
Newhaven	9:45	11:45	9:45	10:45	11:45
White Sand Bay — ARRIVE	9:48	11:48	9:48	10:48	11:48

Ticket Price: Gray City to White Sand Bay One-way: $7 Return: $12

*Passengers can buy tickets on the bus or at the Gray City Bus Station ticket office.

» bus stop

Questions

1. What do we know from this reading?
   a. The distance from Gray City to White Sand Bay.
   b. What the weather will be like at White Sand Bay.
   c. When and where the bus to White Sand Bay picks up passengers.
   d. What fun things there are to do when you get to White Sand Bay.

2. I get on the bus at Long Street at 10:35. At what time will I get to White Sand Bay?
   a. 11:35.   b. 11:48.   c. 11:45.   d. 11:20.

3. What is "White Sand Bay"?
   a. A museum.   b. A movie.   c. A beach.   d. A restaurant.

4. I get on the bus at Gray City Bus Station at 9:30. What day is it?
   a. Saturday.   b. Monday.   c. Thursday.   d. Friday.

5. What most likely happens after September 30?
   a. Return tickets aren't available.   b. The bus times change.
   c. Tickets double in price.   d. You can't buy tickets on the bus.

« bus

19 Comfortable in Your Own Skin

> ⌃ Beauty comes from inside us.

⌃ Yves Saint Laurent (Right)
(cc by Victor Soto)

Every time we open a magazine, we see pictures of beautiful people wearing expensive clothes. **We want to look like the people on the pages**. It's easy to believe that buying those clothes will make us happy. But is the
5   style right for YOU?

Our clothes say a lot about us, so pick yours carefully! The dressmaker Yves Saint Laurent said, "Fashions come and go, but style is forever." He meant that people are more important than clothes. When you're **comfortable**
10   **in your own skin**, you will always look good.

If your jeans cost a lot of money, you will worry about dropping your juice. If your shoes hurt your feet, you'll be unhappy all day. It doesn't matter if your clothes are fashionable or not. Beauty comes from inside us, so
15   choose clothes that make you feel great.

Questions

_____ 1. What can we learn from the reading?

    a. You should be careful when you are wearing something expensive.

    b. Beautiful people wearing expensive clothes help sell magazines.

    c. You don't have to buy expensive clothes to look good.

    d. The people in magazines are not always beautiful.

_____ 2. What was Yves Saint Laurent's job?

    a. He made clothes.   **b.** He made shoes.

    c. He wrote for magazines.   **d.** He drew pictures for magazines.

_____ 3. If you are "**comfortable in your own skin**," how do you feel?

    a. Scared about getting old.   **b.** Happy about yourself.

    c. Proud of your work.   **d.** Surprised about some news.

_____ 4. What might happen if you wear expensive clothes?

    a. People will ask to take a photo of you.

    b. You will want to buy more and more.

    c. People will want to be friends with you.

    d. You will be afraid to get them dirty.

_____ 5. What do we know from the sentence "**We want to look like the people on the pages**"?

    a. People want to buy fashion magazines.

    b. People think nice clothes make them look cool.

    c. People are interested in making new clothes.

    d. People believe reading is very important.

» jeans

« dressmaker

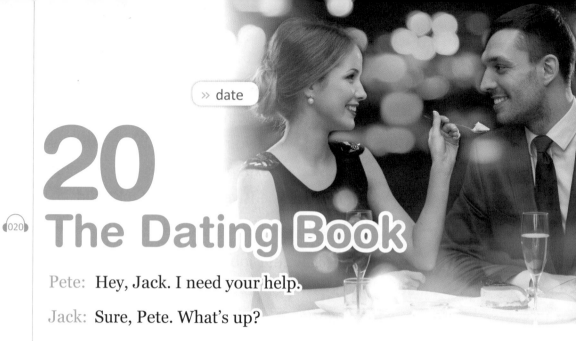

20
The Dating Book

Pete: Hey, Jack. I need your help.

Jack: Sure, Pete. What's up?

Pete: I asked Katherine out on a date, and she said yes.

I'm taking her to dinner this Saturday.

5   Jack: Well, that's great! Why do you need my help?

Pete: The thing is, I'm terrible at dates.

And **I don't want to mess this one up**.

Questions

_____ 1. What can we learn from the conversation?

    a. Pete needs some tips for his date.

    b. Pete is Jack's brother.

    c. Jack owns lots of books on dating.

    d. Katherine is Jack's classmate.

_____ 2. What does it mean when Pete says, "**I don't want to mess this one up**"?

    a. He doesn't want to spend too much money.

    b. He doesn't want the date to be a success.

    c. He doesn't want to make a mistake.

    d. He doesn't want Katherine to think he likes her.

_____ 3. Pete is taking Katherine on a date this Saturday. Which part of the book should he read before taking her out?

    a. Chapter I   **b.** Chapter III   **c.** Chapter II   **d.** The Introduction

Jack: So you need some tips?

Pete: Exactly.

10 Jack: I'll tell you what: I'll lend you my dating book.

Pete: What's that?

Jack: It's this cool book that tells you what to do on dates.

Pete: Thanks so much, man. You're the best.

Contents

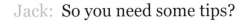
⌃ pick up the check

_____4. How long is the section "**Getting Her Number**"?

   a. Eleven pages. **b.** Ten pages.

   c. Fifteen pages. **d.** Thirteen pages.

_____5. In which part of the book would you most likely find these sentences?

> When dating, it's important not to be the same as every other guy. So for your second date, you should do something special. Take your date somewhere exciting and unusual.

   a. A Date with a Difference. **b.** Calling Her.

   c. Picking Up the Check. **d.** Making Her Wait.

21 Online Shopping Customer Service

shoes4u.com

Thank you for shopping at shoes4u.com. We hope you like your new shoes! However, if there's a problem with your order, please let us know. We'll try to fix **it** as soon as possible.

What's the problem?

5 **Q:** **I made an order, but my shoes didn't arrive.**

A: Send us an email (help@shoes4u.com). Tell us your name and order number, and we'll send you another pair.

Q: **I ordered the wrong size.**

A: Just return the shoes to us within 14 days, and we'll send

10 the correct size. The address is at the bottom of this page.

Q: **I changed my mind. I want my money back.**

A: Sorry; we can't give your money back! But you can choose a different pair of shoes from our website.

For any other problems, call us at 080-465-0099.

15 Someone will be happy to help you.

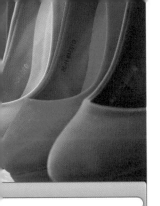

Questions

_____ 1. What does the reading tell us?

    a. It's dangerous to shop online.

    b. We should know how to make an order.

    c. Shoes are very important in daily life.

    d. How to use a shopping website.

_____ 2. What can you do if your order doesn't arrive?

    a. Write a letter.   **b.** Send an email.

    c. Go to an office.   **d.** Make a call.

_____ 3. What does "it" mean?

    a. A problem.   **b.** A website.

    c. A pair of shoes.   **d.** An email.

_____ 4. Your new shoes are too big. Which one is true?

    a. You have two weeks to return them.

    b. You can have your money back.

    c. You can't change the size.

    d. You should send a new order.

_____ 5. If I "changed my mind," what did I do?

    a. Got a headache.   **b.** Started to cry.

    c. Bought something.   **d.** Had a new idea.

22 Right Hand? Left Hand?

⌃ Indian people don't eat with the left hand.

⌃ wipe

Adjit: Thanks for coming to visit me, Mary.

Mary: No; thank you for inviting me.

I can't believe I'm finally visiting India.

Adjit: You must be hungry after your flight.

5 Let's go somewhere to eat.

Mary: Great. You know how much I love Indian food.

Later . . .

Mary: Yum! This is so tasty.

Adjit: **Hold on a second**, Mary.

10 Mary: What is it?

Adjit: You're eating with your left hand.

Mary: Yes. Is there something wrong?

Adjit: It's just that, in India, we don't eat with the left

hand.

>> Indian food

15 Mary: How come?

Adjit: Because here people usually use their left hand to wipe their

bottom after going to the bathroom.

Mary: Oh, I see. So, it's more polite to use the right hand.

Adjit: That's correct.

20 Mary: Then I guess passing people things with the left hand is rude, too?

Adjit: Ha ha! Yes. You learn fast.

Questions

_____ 1. What do we learn about in this conversation?
 a. Adjit's favorite restaurant.   **b.** Eating habits in India.
 c. The history of India.   **d.** Adjit's family.

_____ 2. Which of the following is true?
 a. In India, it's rude to pass things to other people.
 b. Mary is used to the taste of Indian food.
 c. People in India usually eat with their left hand.
 d. Adjit did not want Mary to come to India.

_____ 3. When Adjit and Mary start eating, Adjit tells Mary to "**hold on a second.**" What does he mean?
 a. Can you wait for me?   **b.** Don't eat so fast.
 c. Stop what you're doing.   **d.** Don't hang up the phone.

_____ 4. You're in India on vacation and you buy something in a shop. How do you hand over the money?
 a. With your left hand.   **b.** With your right hand.
 c. With both hands.   **d.** With a special tool.

_____ 5. What can we guess about Mary from the conversation?
 a. She wants to move to India.   **b.** One of her parents is Indian.
 c. It's her first time abroad.   **d.** She writes with her left hand.

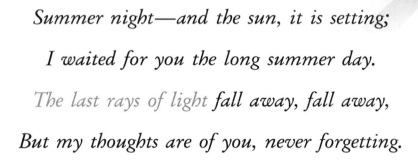

23 Summer Night

⌃ pale

Summer Night

Summer night—and the sun, it is setting;

I waited for you the long summer day.

The last rays of light fall away, fall away,

But my thoughts are of you, never forgetting.

5　The night air is gentle, and gently it plays

The song of a summer I fear now is ending.

Summer night—and the sun, it is setting;

I waited for you the long summer day.

In the sky hangs the moon, a ghost pale and gray,

10　In place of the sun that once was there shining.

And my memories are moons, and my hopes,

they are fading.

My sun, you are gone. And I, alone, must stay.

Summer night—and the sun, it is setting;

15　I waited for you the long summer day.

« fade

Questions

_____ 1. What is the poem about?

  a. Having fun during summer vacation.

  b. How beautiful the moon is.

  c. Starting on a long trip.

  d. Something coming to an end.

_____ 2. How does the poet describe the moon?

  a. Like the sun.   b. Like a woman.

  c. Like a child.   d. Like a ghost.

_____ 3. What does "**The last rays of light**" mean?

  a. The poet's thoughts.   b. The moon.

  c. The night air.   d. The sun.

_____ 4. Why does the writer keep saying, "I waited for you"?

  a. He's afraid of time running out.

  b. He wants his love to return to him.

  c. He needs someone to help him.

  d. He doesn't like it when people are late.

_____ 5. Which picture best fits the poem?

  a.    b.

  c.    d.

» universal choking sign

24 First Aid for Choking

I took a first aid course last week. We learned how to help people in trouble. One of the things we learned was how to help someone who is choking. Our teacher gave us a useful sheet to help us remember the steps. Here's what she gave us:

FIRST AID FOR CHOKING

Signs that a person might be choking:

- **The person cannot breathe, cough, or speak.**
- **The person makes an "I'm choking" sign with his or her hands.**
- **The person's lips turn blue.**

Questions

_____ 1. What can we learn from the reading?

    a. How to stay healthy.   **b.** How to use sign language.

    c. How to save someone's life.   **d.** How to cross the road safely.

_____ 2. If someone is choking, which of the following can't he or she do?

    a. Move his or her arms.   **b.** Say, "I'm choking."

    c. Nod his or her head.   **d.** Close his or her hands.

_____ 3. Which of the following is a "belly button"?

    a.   **b.**   **c.**   **d.**

  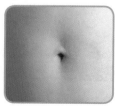 

Step 1.   Ask, "Are you choking?"

Step 2.   If the person signs "yes," step behind the person, and put your arms around his or her waist.

Step 3.   Close one hand and hold it with the other. Place your hands just above the person's **belly button**.

Step 4.   Pull sharply towards yourself.

Step 5.   Repeat until the object comes out or the person can breathe.

_____ 4.   You think someone is choking. According to the reading, what's the first thing you should do?

    a. Put your arms around his or her waist.

    b. Close one hand and hold it with the other.

    c. Ask him or her if they're choking.

    d. Step behind him or her.

_____ 5.   Which of the following is a sign that someone's choking?

    a.   **b.**   **c.**   **d.**

  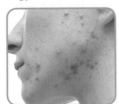 

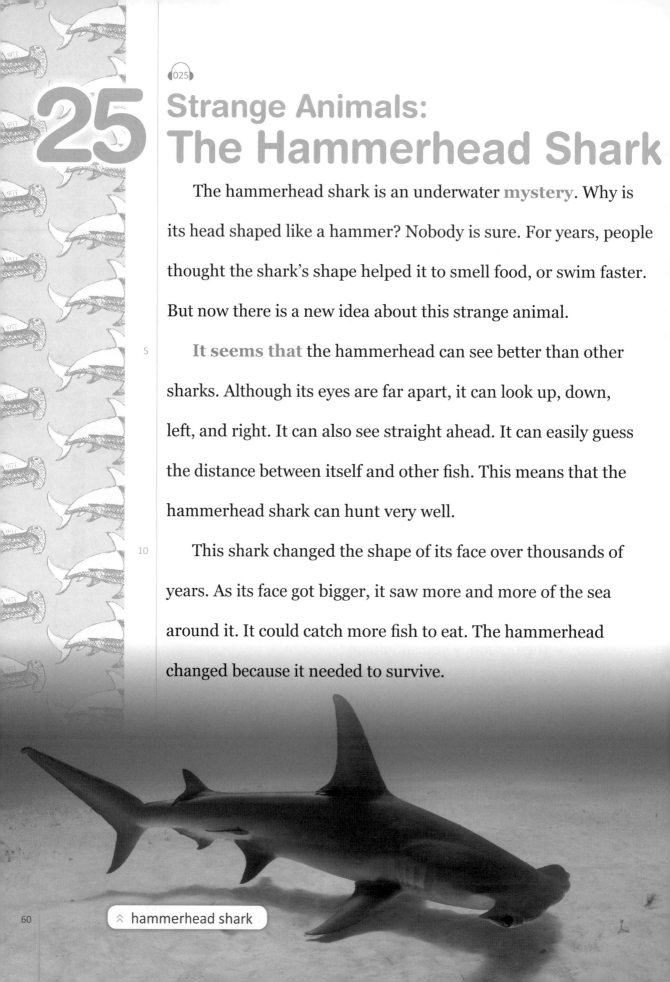

25

Strange Animals: The Hammerhead Shark

The hammerhead shark is an underwater **mystery**. Why is its head shaped like a hammer? Nobody is sure. For years, people thought the shark's shape helped it to smell food, or swim faster. But now there is a new idea about this strange animal.

5   **It seems that** the hammerhead can see better than other sharks. Although its eyes are far apart, it can look up, down, left, and right. It can also see straight ahead. It can easily guess the distance between itself and other fish. This means that the hammerhead shark can hunt very well.

10   This shark changed the shape of its face over thousands of years. As its face got bigger, it saw more and more of the sea around it. It could catch more fish to eat. The hammerhead changed because it needed to survive.

⌃ hammerhead shark

˅ Stingrays are a particular favorite of the hammerhead sharks.

˅ The hammerhead can see better than other sharks.

Questions

_____ 1. What do we learn about hammerhead sharks?

    a. Their eyes got bigger over time.

    b. They can't catch enough fish.

    c. They move faster than other sharks.

    d. Their shape helps them to see.

_____ 2. Which one is not mentioned in the reading?

    a. Smelling.   **b.** Resting.   **c.** Hunting.   **d.** Swimming.

_____ 3. What can you say about a "**mystery**"?

    a. It makes a lot of noise.   **b.** It happens very slowly.

    c. It doesn't eat much.   **d.** It's hard to understand.

_____ 4. Which one can hammerhead sharks do?

    a. See things behind them.

    b. Make sounds to help other sharks.

    c. Know how far away things are.

    d. Live in very cold water.

_____ 5. When do we use "**It seems that . . .**"?

    a. When we're talking about things which are different.

    b. When we're talking about things which are the same.

    c. When we think something is true, but we're not sure.

    d. When we know for sure that something is not true.

26 Jim's Calendar

Hi. I'm Jim. I have a very busy life. I work hard, but I also like to do lots of fun activities, so I use a calendar to **keep track of** what I'm doing and when. Take a look at my schedule for March this year.

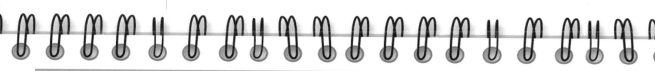

March

Monday	Tuesday	Wednesday	Thursday	Friday	Saturday
1	2	3	4 Big meeting at work (prepare presentation)	5	6 Mom's birthday (send card)
8	9	10 Drinks with the guys at Moonlight 9 p.m.	11 Theater with Jenny	12	13
15	16 Monthly book club meeting 7 p.m.	17		19 Day off work (pack for vacation)	20 Fly to Paris 8:30 a.m.
22	23 Back from Paris	24 Back to work	25 Dinner with Dad at Mario's Restaurant 7:30 p.m.	26	27 Art exhibition (last day)
29	30	31			

Questions

_____ 1. What is Jim's main reason for using a calendar?
   a. To remember birthdays.
   b. To organize his vacations.
   c. To remember dinner dates.
   d. To organize his life.

_____ 2. Where will Jim be on the evening of Wednesday, March 10?
   a. In a bar.
   b. On an airplane.
   c. At the theater.
   d. At a wedding.

_____ 3. What do you do when you "keep track of" things?
   a. Help someone when he or she is in trouble.
   b. Note down anything important.
   c. Break the rules made by your parents.
   d. Go to bed early to keep up your energy.

_____ 4. On what date did Jim most likely take this photo?

   a. Friday, March 19.
   b. Thursday, March 11.
   c. Sunday, March 21.
   d. Tuesday, March 16.

_____ 5. Jim just sent this message. What day is it today?

> Hey, man. Sorry. I'm running late. I'll be at the café in about 10 minutes. Could you order me some pancakes and a coffee?

   a. Sunday, March 14.
   b. Sunday, March 28.
   c. Saturday, March 20.
   d. Thursday, March 23.

Sunday

7
Barbecue
at Jenny's
4 p.m.

14
Brunch with Mike
11 a.m.

21

28
Mary's wedding
(buy gift)

27 The Cold Shoulder

Dear Doris
EACH MONDAY

Doris answers all your teen worries!

Dear Doris,

I have a big problem.

My best friend is **giving me the cold shoulder**. She won't talk to me. When I call her she doesn't pick up. When I try to talk to her in school, she just walks away. The strange thing is, I don't even know why she's doing it! I don't think I did anything to upset her.

What should I do?

**Confused Girl, 17,
Taipei**

Questions

____ 1. Why did the young person write a letter to Doris?
   a. To complain about some bad service.
   b. To say sorry for something she did.
   c. To ask for help with a personal problem.
   d. To find out about a school course.

____ 2. What does Doris tell Confused Girl to do?
   a. Not to mind her friend and forget about her.
   b. Show her friend she cares about her.
   c. Throw a big birthday party for her friend.
   d. Tell her friend to stop being so silly.

____ 3. What do you do if you "**give someone the cold shoulder**"?
   a. You call them all the time.   **b.** You tell them all about yourself.
   c. You buy them a cold drink.   **d.** You avoid them.

>> upset

Dear Confused Girl,

Perhaps she's not mad at you for something you DID do. Perhaps she's mad at you for something you DIDN'T do. Maybe you forgot to get her a birthday gift or ask her how her date went. Sometimes it's the things we don't do that upset people the most. She probably felt ignored herself, so she's trying to make you feel the same way. Show your friend you care about her; she'll soon forget about the whole thing.

Doris

4. How do you think Confused Girl felt when she wrote her letter?

   a. Puzzled.   b. Tired.   c. Scared.   d. Lucky.

5. What does Doris mean by "She'll soon forget about the whole thing"?

   a. "She'll soon forget you."

   b. "She'll soon stop coming to school."

   c. "She'll soon forgive you."

   d. "She'll soon find a new friend."

(028)

• When did you start writing songs and why?

I think when I was about 10 years old. I don't really know why. It just happened naturally.

• How does it feel to be a famous pop star?

5   I love being able to write and perform music for a living. But **on the other hand**, I have no private life anymore!

• What song are you most proud of?

I think I'm most proud of *Love Me More*, my first
10   number one hit. It took a long time to get right, but I'm still really happy with **the end result**, even a few years later.

• What advice would you give to someone who wants to become a performing artist?

15   Make sure people hear your music. The Internet is a great place to do that. After all, I started out posting my songs on YouTube. Now I'm performing my songs for millions of people.

⌃ pop star

⌃ interview

1. What is the interview mainly about?
   a. A musician's life and opinions.
   b. A musician's future plans.
   c. A musician's last concert.
   d. A musician's new album.

2. When did the musician start to write songs?
   a. When she was in high school.
   b. When she was in college.
   c. When she was a young girl.
   d. When she was in kindergarten.

3. Why does the musician use the phrase "on the other hand"?
   a. To express how excited she is.
   b. To express the bad side of something.
   c. To say where something is.
   d. To express how sad she is.

4. How did the musician most likely become famous?
   a. She sent a song to a record company.
   b. A producer visited her high school.
   c. A producer saw her songs online.
   d. Her parents were famous.

5. What is "the end result"?
   a. Performing for millions of people.
   b. Getting a number one hit.
   c. Becoming famous.
   d. The song *Love Me More*.

⌄ private life

29 School Bullying

Tuesday, March 17, 2015

Dear Diary,

Today was a bad day. Jimmy Thompson came up to me again at lunch with his friends. He started calling me names. Then when I tried to walk away, he grabbed me and pushed me to the ground. Then they all started laughing at me. Luckily, a teacher came along before anything worse could happen. Jimmy pretended to help me up. He was pretending that I tripped. And then he said that he'd finish the job tomorrow. Now I'm scared to even go to school. Should I say I'm sick and take a day off? No, then Jimmy will know I'm scared of him. And that's just what he wants. I have to be brave. If I make him think that what he's doing doesn't bother me, maybe he'll stop. It's worth a try, anyway. I'll let you know how things go tomorrow. Wish me luck.

« take a day off   » grab

15

16

22   23   24

Vacation

30

« trip

« school bullying

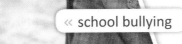uestions

_____1. Why did the writer have a bad day?

    a. A teacher caught him lying.

    b. Someone hurt him.

    c. He got sick.

    d. He lost his lunch money.

_____2. Who is Jimmy Thompson?

    a. The writer's teacher.   **b.** The writer's best friend.

    c. The writer's enemy.   **d.** The writer himself.

_____3. What does "**finish the job**" mean in the reading?

    a. Continue the beating.   **b.** Give a helping hand.

    c. Tell the teacher.   **d.** Stay at home.

_____4. What will the writer most likely do tomorrow?

    a. Stay at home and pretend to be sick.

    b. Go to school and say sorry to Jimmy.

    c. Go to school and act like nothing happened.

    d. Go tell the police about his problem.

_____5. Who is the "**you**" the writer is talking to?

    a. His diary.   **b.** His mom.

    c. The reader.   **d.** His teacher.

30 Berkeley Science Museum

My friends and I are planning on going to the science museum this weekend. We weren't sure how to get there, so we looked on the museum's website for directions.

Berkeley Science Museum (How to Find Us)

By Subway:

Green Line Get off at **Archway Station**. The museum is a five-minute walk from the station.

Orange Line Get off at **City Hall Station**, and take bus number **42B**, **236**, or **53** to Berkeley Science Museum. The buses stop at the museum entrance.

By Car:

From the North: Follow the **M38** south. Turn left onto the **M32**. Turn left onto the **A624**. The museum is on your left.

From the South: Follow the **M32** north. Turn right onto the **A624**. The museum is on your left.

By Bus:

Buses stopping at Berkeley Science Museum leave from Berkeley West Bus Station (53, 21, 34), City Hall Subway Station (42B, 236, 53), and the Prince Hotel (21, 34). To download a full timetable, click here.

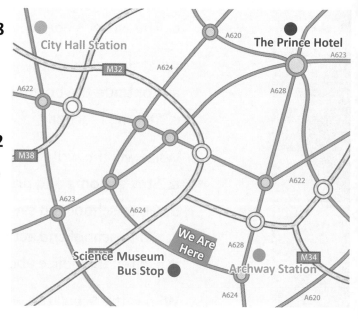

<< bus

>> museum

Questions

_____ 1. What are the map and directions mainly for?

   a. To help people get to Berkeley West Bus Station.

   b. To help people get to the Prince Hotel.

   c. To help people get to Berkeley Science Museum.

   d. To help people get to City Hall Station.

_____ 2. Where can I catch the number 53 bus?

   a. At Berkley West Bus Station only.

   b. At City Hall Subway Station only.

   c. At the Prince Hotel and City Hall Subway Station.

   d. At Berkeley West Bus Station and City Hall Subway Station.

_____ 3. What is "**A624**"?

   a. A station.   b. A bus.   c. A road.   d. A subway line.

_____ 4. Which of the following will appear if I click on the word "**here**" in the final sentence?

a.

Service Number 21		
STOP	TIME	TIME
Berkeley West Bus Station	8:30	9:30

b.

Tuesday – Friday: 9:00 – 17:30
Saturday: 8:30 – 18:30
Sunday – Monday: Closed

c.

Information desk
Tel. (02) 6457 4765
@: information@berkeleyscimuseum.net

d.

May 19: Special Talk by
         Dr. Richard North
May 30: Children's Fun Day
June 15: All Tickets Half-Price

_____ 5. Which of the following is not shown on the map?

   a. Berkeley Science Museum.   b. The Prince Hotel.

   c. Archway Subway Station.   d. Berkeley West Bus Station.

31

Can Dogs See in Color ?

by Jeff James

>> Dogs are colorblind.

Lots of people think that dogs see in black and white. But this is not true. Scientists recently discovered that dogs do see colors, just not quite the same colors that we **do**.

When people see a rainbow, they see purple, blue, blue-green, green, yellow, orange, and red. But when dogs see a rainbow, they see gray, blue, gray, yellow-brown, yellow, and yellow-brown. Can you imagine?

Dogs see red and green as a single color (yellow-brown) and also blue-green and purple as a single color (gray). This means that if you buy your dog a bright red toy, it will see it as an ugly **yellowish** brown.

⌄ detect

Why? Well, a human eye has three different types of cells that can detect color. Dogs' eyes, however, have just two. This makes the range of colors that they can pick up much more limited.

⌃ rainbow

Questions

_____ 1. What is the article about?

    a. How to treat dogs.

    b. How dogs see the world.

    c. What best to feed your dog.

    d. Why exercise is important for dogs.

_____ 2. My dog has a purple toy. What color does he see the toy as?

    a. Gray.   **b.** Red.   **c.** Yellow-brown.   **d.** Blue.

_____ 3. What does "**do**" mean in the reading?

    a. Imagine.   **b.** Discover.   **c.** Detect.   **d.** Think.

_____ 4. Which colors do dogs see the same as humans?

    a. Purple and blue.   **b.** Blue and yellow.

    c. Orange and yellow.   **d.** Orange and purple.

_____ 5. What does "**yellowish**" mean?

    a. Bright yellow.   **b.** Not yellow.

    c. Kind of yellow.   **d.** Too yellow.

032

32
A Job Opening

resume

Job Opportunities

Pierre's Restaurant is a popular French restaurant in the city center famous for its excellent French cooking. We are very proud of our high-quality food and service. Right now we are looking for two new people to join our team.

· ·

Position: Cook (full-time)

You should:

- have at least four years' cooking experience in a good restaurant
- have a good knowledge of French food and cooking techniques
- be willing to work long hours
- **enjoy working as part of a team**

We offer: • NT$30,000—40,000 a month

  • two days off a week

· ·

Position: Waiter/Waitress (weekends only)

You should: • be friendly   • be hard-working   • be willing to learn
No experience needed.

We offer: • NT$130 an hour to start

If interested, please send your resume to pierre@webmail.com.tw.

Questions

_____ 1. What is the point of this piece?

   a. To teach you how to make a dish.

   b. To tell people about a new place to eat.

   c. To find new workers for a restaurant.

   d. To invite people to a dinner party.

_____ 2. What is true about the waiter/waitress position?

   a. It's for students only.

   b. Only people with experience can apply.

   c. It's a part-time position.

   d. The pay is $130 per day.

_____ 3. What does "**You should enjoy working as part of a team**" mean?

   a. You will be your own boss.

   b. You will be responsible for a group of people.

   c. You will be working closely with others.

   d. You will have to talk to the customers.

Four people wanted the cook position. These are the notes that the boss made about them.

Name	Experience
Kyle	6 years as cook at Mario's Italian Restaurant
Andy	4 years cooking burgers in a fast food restaurant
Lisa	5 years as a cook at Louie's French Café & Restaurant
Judy	No work experience; 3 years of cooking school in Paris

_____ 4. Who would most likely get the job?

   a. Kyle.   **b.** Andy.   **c.** Lisa.   **d.** Judy.

_____ 5. What do you write on a resume?

   a. Your food order.   **b.** Your work history.

   c. Your thoughts.   **d.** Your thanks.

33 Enjoy Nature

Cities can be loud and crowded. You can hear horns beeping and garbage trucks passing by. You hear people talking and babies crying on the bus. At night, there are lights everywhere—from cars, stores, restaurants, and apartments. Do you ever just want to leave?

5   If you are seeking peace and quiet, you can find it easily. Why not pack a picnic and take a hike through the woods? If you are close to a beach, why not take off your shoes and walk in the sand? Nature can be found in city environments, too. Most cities have parks with grass, trees, and flowers. You can even bring a book to read on a park bench.

10   Even if you are very busy, take time to **stop and smell the roses**. Nature is here for us all to enjoy, and the best part is it's free!

⌄ take a hike

» garbage truck

Questions

_____ 1. What is this reading mainly saying?

    a. Enjoying nature is a good way to find peace and quiet.

    b. There are many different things to do outside the city.

    c. Cities are loud and crowded places.

    d. There are lots of free things to do in the city.

_____ 2. In the reading, what does the writer
say is the best thing about nature?

    a. You can enjoy it while having a picnic.

    b. You can feel sand on your feet.

    c. It doesn't cost anything.

    d. It can be found on the beach.

_____ 3. What does it mean to "**stop and smell the roses**"?

    a. To plant roses in your garden and enjoy them.

    b. To take a break and enjoy the simple things in life.

    c. To buy flowers and keep them in your home.

    d. To find a beautiful flower garden and read.

_____ 4. Why are cities loud and crowded?

    a. There are lots of people living there.

    b. You can bring a book to read in a park.

    c. People in the city like to talk.

    d. Not a lot of people take a hike through the woods.

_____ 5. Where does the writer say you can find peace?

    a. Anywhere outside the city.

    b. On buses and in cars.

    c. In stores.

    d. Inside and outside the city.

» park bench

(034)

Homemade food

Secondhand clothes

FLEA MARKET THIS SATURDAY

CDs & DVDs

Old books

SIGN UP AS A SELLER AT
www.hanovermarket.com
$5 per table, per period
Time periods:
9:00–13:00 / 13:00–17:00

Art objects

From 9:00 a.m. to 5:00 p.m. this Saturday (5/9), there will be a flea market in the town square. Everyone is welcome! If you have things to sell, you can sign up as a seller online. Or just come and see if anything catches your eye!

Are you an artist? Then why not sell your paintings?

Are you a baker? Then why not sell your cakes?

Do you have lots of "junk" you want to throw away?

One man's junk is another man's treasure!

So come on down and have a great day out!

Buyers enter free of charge!

1. Which of the pictures shows the event described in the reading?

a.

b.

c.

d.

2. Where will the event be?
   a. In the town hall.
   b. In someone's yard.
   c. In the town square.
   d. On the beach.

3. How do you feel about something that "**catches your eye**"?
   a. You don't like its color.
   b. You think it's a waste of money.
   c. You're interested in it.
   d. You want to return it.

4. I want to sell some of my old clothes at the event. How much will I have to pay to set up a table from 9 a.m. to 5 p.m.?
   a. $10.
   b. $5.
   c. $15.
   d. Nothing.

5. What does the poster tell people by saying "**One man's junk is another man's treasure!**"?
   a. You'll get in trouble if you attend the event.
   b. Everyone has something he or she can sell at the event.
   c. The items at the event will be very expensive.
   d. You must keep the area clean and tidy.

» slam dunk

« basketball

35 Basketball

(035)

What do a peach basket and a soccer ball have in common? Would you ever guess basketball? In 1891, **the game of basketball was born**. It was invented by a Canadian man, James Naismith. He created it to keep athletes active inside during long winters.

⌃ James Naismith (1861–1939)

The game has changed a lot over the years. The peach basket was replaced with a hoop, which made the game faster. This way, the game didn't have to stop so the ball could be gotten out of the basket. The early game was played with a soccer ball. Later, a special ball was created for the game.

By the late 1800s, basketball was being played across Canada and the United States. It was a popular sport taught in high schools and colleges. Today, basketball is played all over the world. It is one of the most popular games ever invented.

Questions

_____ 1. What is this reading mainly telling us?
   a. There are many rules in basketball.
   b. Basketball has an interesting history.
   c. Basketball is the most popular sport.
   d. James Naismith was a smart man.

_____ 2. What does "**the game of basketball was born**" mean in the reading?
   a. People stopped playing basketball.
   b. People started playing basketball.
   c. Basketball was popular.
   d. Basketball was unusual.

_____ 3. Why did the game have to stop so the ball could be gotten out of the peach basket?
   a. The players needed a break.
   b. So the game would go faster.
   c. It made the game last longer.
   d. The ball couldn't fall through it.

_____ 4. What is one reason why James Naismith invented basketball?
   a. He wanted to make money.
   b. It was too cold to exercise outside.
   c. He didn't really like soccer.
   d. It was a very popular game.

_____ 5. What is one change that was made to the game after it was invented?
   a. The game became slower.
   b. A player had to get the ball out of the basket.
   c. The peach basket became more popular.
   d. A soccer ball was no longer used.

36. King Henry VIII

(036)

King Henry VIII is one of England's most famous kings. He was a strong military leader, but also a talented poet and musician. However, he is probably most famous for his six

5 marriages. Below is a timeline of Henry's busy love life.

Catherine gave birth to a daughter, Mary.

Henry ordered that Anne's head be cut off. After Anne was dead, Henry married Jane Seymour.

» Jane Seymour

Henry was born.

1491	1509	1516	1533	1536	1537	1540

Henry became King of England and married Catherine of Aragon, his dead brother's wife.

⌄ Catherine of Aragon

Henry divorced Catherine and married Anne Boleyn. Anne gave birth to a daughter, Elizabeth.

⌄ Anne Boleyn

Jane died giving birth to a son, Edward.

Henry married Anne of Cleves, but divorced **her** almost immediately as she was too ugly. He then married Catherine Howard.

» Anne of Cleves

« Henry VIII

Henry ordered that Catherine Howard's head be cut off.

Henry married Catherine Parr.

| 1542 | 1543 | 1547 |

Henry died.

1. What is the main focus of the timeline?
   a. Henry VIII's poetry.
   b. Henry VIII''s wars.
   c. Henry VIII''s marriages.
   d. Henry VIII''s children.

2. What happened to Henry's second and fifth wives?
   a. They died giving birth.
   b. They were killed.
   c. They ran away.
   d. They died of old age.

3. Who is "**her**"?
   a. Anne Boleyn.
   b. Catherine Howard.
   c. Anne of Cleves.
   d. Jane Seymour.

4. According to the timeline, who was born last?
   a. Edward.   b. Elizabeth.
   c. Mary.   d. Henry.

5. Which of the following happened after the death of Catherine Howard?
   a. Henry's brother died.
   b. Henry married Anne Boleyn.
   c. Henry became king of England.
   d. Henry married Catherine Parr.

(037)

OCEANIA
Working Holiday Visa

Have the time of your life . . .

Every year thousands of young people visit Oceania on working holiday visas.

With a working holiday visa you can:

- Travel freely in Oceania for one year.
- Work whenever you want to support your travels.
- Study for up to six months.

Only people between the ages of 18 and 30 can apply for working holiday visas.

To know more about working holiday visas and how to apply, visit **www.oceania.gov.oc**

> I had such a great time. The only bad thing was having to go home at the end!
>
> Joe, 27, London

> Do it! It'll change your life! What an amazing adventure!
>
> Mike, 22, Taipei

> I met so many interesting people and made lots of new friends.
>
> Gail, 25, New York

» koala

Questions

_____ 1. Who is the reading mainly for?
- **a.** Young people who want to travel abroad.
- **b.** Middle-aged people who want to find work.
- **c.** Old people who are about to stop working.
- **d.** Middle school students who are studying geography.

_____ 2. How long can you stay in Oceania on a working holiday visa?
- **a.** Six months.
- **b.** Six weeks.
- **c.** One year.
- **d.** One year and six months.

_____ 3. If you had "the time of your life," what kind of experience did you have?
- **a.** A boring one.
- **b.** A fun one.
- **c.** A lonely one.
- **d.** A tiring one.

_____ 4. What did Gail from New York love most about her time in Oceania?
- **a.** The sights.
- **b.** The culture.
- **c.** The food.
- **d.** The people.

_____ 5. What does it mean to "support your travels"?
- **a.** Take lots of pictures so you can remember your travels.
- **b.** Write a blog so people can share your travels.
- **c.** Make money so you can pay for your travels.
- **d.** Be careful so you don't get hurt on your travels.

(038)

≪ high-quality items

○ ○ ○   Wise Wally's Daily Blog

◀ ▶ ＋ ▢

📖 ▦   Apple   Yahoo!   Google Maps   YouTube   Wikipedia   News (1002)▾   Popular▾

Wise Wally's Daily Blog

WISE WORDS EVERY DAY OF THE WEEK

Wise Wally's Top Tips for Using Your Money Wisely

Posted by Wise Wally on April 19, 2015

Hello, readers! We all know that money doesn't grow on trees, so here are some things you can do to make your dollars last.

1. Pay a little more.

Don't be afraid to pay a little extra for high-quality items. Cheap

5　goods often wear out or break quickly. Pay a little more, and you'll save money in the long run.

2. Wait for sales.

Do you really need that new summer dress right now? Wait until the fall and you'll get it for half the price. You can always wear it next

10　summer.

3. Buy secondhand.

You can pick up some great stuff in secondhand shops and markets these days—books for school, clothes, DVDs, everything. You'll be surprised what treasures you can find!

Questions

_____ 1. What is the main aim of Wise Wally's blog?
- **a.** To make people laugh.
- **b.** To give people tips.
- **c.** To report the news.
- **d.** To make money.

_____ 2. Which of the following can we learn from the blog?
- **a.** Never buy secondhand goods.
- **b.** Paying more can save you money.
- **c.** Cheap items last for a long time.
- **d.** Never wait to buy an item you like.

≫ wear out

_____ 3. What does the writer mean by "money doesn't grow on trees"?
- **a.** Money isn't healthy.
- **b.** Money isn't useful.
- **c.** Money isn't easy to get.
- **d.** Money isn't a fruit.

≫ sale

_____ 4. What might be number 4 on Wally's list?
- **a.** Buy a car.
- **b.** Learn another language.
- **c.** Take a vacation.
- **d.** Eat at home.

≫ secondhand market

_____ 5. What does "treasures" mean in the final paragraph?
- **a.** Good used items.
- **b.** Works of art.
- **c.** Bags of money.
- **d.** New ideas.

Dog-Walking Service

Too busy to walk your dog?
Then let us do **it** for you!

Did you know most dogs need 30-60 minutes of exercise per day to stay healthy and happy? But if you have a full-time job or kids, it can be hard to find that much free time.

That's what we're here for!

Our team of dog walkers will make sure your dog gets the best workout possible—and has a lot of fun, too!

You can set up a regular session or, for dog-walking emergencies, call us on short notice. We can be there to walk your dog within two hours!

So the next time your **four-legged friend** needs some exercise, give us a call!

Regular service: $10/hr.

Emergency service (less than 12 hrs. notice): $15/hr.

HAPPY PUPPY DOG-WALKING SERVICE
078-897-347
happypuppy@webmail.com

Questions

_____ **1.** What is the writer offering to do?

    a. Train your dog for you.

    b. Take care of your sick dog.

    c. Exercise your dog for you.

    d. Look after your dog while you're on vacation.

_____ **2.** It's 2 p.m. now. When can someone from the company be here to help me?

    a. Before 4 p.m.   **b.** At 5 p.m.

    c. Tomorrow morning.   **d.** The day after tomorrow.

_____ **3.** What does the phrase "**four-legged friend**" mean?

    a. Dog walker.   **b.** Dog.

    c. Dog owner.   **d.** Dog lover.

_____ **4.** Which of the following people most likely uses the service?

    a.

    b.

    c.

    d.

_____ **5.** What does "**it**" mean in the reading?

    a. Walk your dog.   **b.** Have a lot of fun.

    c. Call on short notice.   **d.** Find free time.

⌃ cartoon

» Young people love to play video games.

40 Are Video Games Really Dangerous?

040

Young people love to play video games. It's a fact of life. Another fact of life is that, sometimes, young people do bad things. And whenever a young person does something terrible, like hurt someone seriously, people have to blame something. In the past it was cartoons, action

5 movies, and even rock music. These days, people blame video games.

But does playing a video game really make people act differently? A recent study seems to suggest **so**. First, scientists asked a group of students to play a video game. Some played as heroes; others played as bad guys. Later, the scientists asked the students to either reward or

10 punish a stranger. The "heroes" preferred to reward the strangers (by giving them chocolate), but the "bad guys" preferred to punish the strangers (by making them eat hot sauce). This shows that **even a little gaming** can change the way you treat others in real life.

» action movie

punish

Are Video Games Really Dangerous?

Questions

_____ 1. What point is the writer trying to make?

 a. A lot of young people like to play video games.

 b. Playing video games can influence your actions.

 c. People often blame video games for bad things.

 d. You should always help strangers.

_____ 2. What is true about the study?

 a. Scientists asked students to play a board game.

 b. All of the students who took part played as bad guys.

 c. Some students made strangers eat hot sauce.

 d. Only people who liked chocolate could take part.

_____ 3. What does "**so**" mean in the reading?

 a. Young people love to play video games.

 b. People have to blame something.

 c. Young people sometimes do bad things.

 d. Playing video games affects people's actions.

_____ 4. What does the writer probably think?

 a. Young people should avoid playing video games.

 b. Young people should watch more cartoons.

 c. It's okay for adults to play video games but not children.

 d. Young people shouldn't listen to rock music.

_____ 5. What does the writer mean by the phrase "**even a little gaming**"?

 a. Playing no video games at all.

 b. Playing children's video games.

 c. Playing video games for a short time.

 d. Playing video games when you're young.

91

41 | Sundae Recipe

Some friends are coming over later to hang out. We're going to watch a movie, talk, and eat LOTS of ice cream. In fact, I'm going to make them one of my favorite treats: chocolate-banana sundaes. They're really delicious, and

5   they're super easy and fast to make; you can throw one together in **two shakes of a lamb's tail**. Here's the recipe. Now you can make some for your friends, too!

⌃ vanilla ice cream

⌃ sprinkles

Chocolate-Banana Sundae Recipe

Serves 4 | Time to make: 5 minutes

Ingredients

- 4 small bananas
- 1 bottle of chocolate sauce
- 1 pot of vanilla ice cream
- 1/4 cup of sprinkles

Directions

Step 1: Peel the bananas.

Step 2: Cut the bananas into slices.

Step 3: Divide the ice cream among four bowls.

Step 4: Put the bananas on top of the ice cream.

Step 5: Pour some chocolate sauce over the ice cream and the bananas.

Step 6: Toss the sprinkles over everything.

Step 7: Pick up a spoon and start eating!

>> peel the banana

⌃ bowl

>> sauce

Questions

_____ 1. What does the reading teach you how to do?

   a. Make a dessert.   **b.** Make ice cream.

   c. Make chocolate.   **d.** Make a bowl.

_____ 2. I have all the items ready to make the dish. Which picture shows the items that I need?

   a.    **b.**    **c.**    **d.**

_____ 3. What does it mean to do something in "two shakes of a lamb's tail"?

   a. You do it with difficulty.

   b. You do it very quickly.

   c. You do it with lots of mistakes.

   d. You do it even though you don't want to.

_____ 4. Which of the following should do you do first according to the recipe?

   a. Share out the ice cream.   **b.** Add the sprinkles.

   c. Peel the bananas.   **d.** Add the chocolate sauce.

_____ 5. How long would it take to make sundaes for eight people?

   a. Ten minutes.   **b.** Twenty minutes.

   c. Five minutes.   **d.** Two and a half minutes.

42 | Traveling Abroad With the Family

⌃ London

⌃ Buckingham Palace

⌃ Edinburgh

I just got back from my first-ever trip abroad—one whole week in the United Kingdom! I went with my parents, my two brothers, and my Aunt Winnie. We spent the first few days in London. **We took in all the sights** and went to some great museums, too. We even visited Buckingham Palace, where the Queen of England lives!

From London, we took a train all the way up to Edinburgh in Scotland. The best thing about Edinburgh was the castle, no question about it. Aunt Winnie took about a million photos in front of it. And we had haggis in Edinburgh, too. Haggis is a sheep's stomach filled with the sheep's heart, liver, and lungs! It might sound a little bit scary, but the taste wasn't so bad. My family and I had a lot of fun during the trip. I can't wait for the next one!

» haggis

Questions

1. What is the reading mainly about?
   a. The writer's family vacation.   b. The Queen of England.
   c. How to make haggis.   d. Castles in Scotland.

2. What is said in the reading?
   a. The writer stayed with the queen.
   b. The writer drank lots of English tea.
   c. The writer visited two cities.
   d. The writer went to Edinburgh by bus.

3. What does the writer mean by saying, "We took in all the sights"?
   a. We saw all the interesting places.
   b. We bought lots of cool gifts.
   c. We stayed away from crowded areas.
   d. We stayed inside most of the time.

4. What is likely true about Aunt Winnie?
   a. She was too scared to try haggis.
   b. Edinburgh Castle was her favorite place.
   c. The queen agreed to take a picture with her.
   d. Traveling on the train made her sick.

5. A kind man took a photo of the whole family at the airport.
   Which of these is that photo?

   a.    b.

   c.    d.

43 Why Should We Read?

⌃ Internet

When I say reading, I don't mean quickly looking over a blog or reading your texts. There's a big difference, you see, between that type of reading and real reading—getting lost in a good book. The type of reading I'm talking about has a
5　lot of benefits. When you read a book, all your attention is on the story. This lowers stress and builds your powers of concentration and memory. Now think about how you feel when you're reading something on the Internet. Your attention may be on the article one minute, but the next minute you're
10　checking your email, laughing at a funny picture, or watching a video about cats. **Your focus is all over the place**. Try to find at least 15 to 20 minutes a day to quietly read a book. You'll be surprised how much **it** can change your life.

⌃ blog

》 Reading can change your life.

Questions

1. What is the writer's main point?

   a. There are two types of reading.

   b. It's not easy to focus when on the Internet.

   c. Reading can help lower stress.

   d. People should read more books.

2. What does the article say about "real reading"?

   a. It helps develop your mind.

   b. It makes you a more caring person.

   c. It makes you less able to focus.

   d. It helps you see better.

3. What is "it"?

   a. Looking over a blog.   **b.** Checking your email.

   c. Reading a book.   **d.** Watching a video.

4. What is likely true about the writer?

   a. He doesn't like Internet videos of cats.

   b. He reads for at least 15 minutes a day.

   c. He doesn't use email.

   d. He uses the Internet for less than 15 minutes a day.

5. What does the writer mean by "Your focus is all over the place"?

   a. You're doing too many things at once.

   b. You can't find what you're looking for.

   c. You're taking too much time to finish something.

   d. You're doing something the correct way.

44 Why Do Whales Explode?

Here on the shores of southern Canada, a whale is dying.

After trying for hours to save the whale, the rescue team is giving up hope.

5   Soon the team will face a new problem, because when a whale dies, it becomes **a time bomb**.

As the animal begins to rot, gases build up inside it. The team must find a way to free 10 these gases, or the whale will explode!

This film from Ireland from 2012 shows how to deal with a whale that's about to **pop**.

Locals found this dead whale on a beach, already full of dangerous gas.

15   With the whale almost ready to burst, the rescue team acted quickly.

They cut hundreds of small holes in the whale's body, and little by little they brought down the pressure.

Back in Canada, the whale has died, and the rescue team quickly 20 **gets to work**.

⌃ rescue team

⌃ explode

Questions

_____ 1. What do we learn from the TV show?
  a. How to stop a dead whale from exploding.
  b. How to save a dying whale.
  c. Why some whales wash up on the shore.
  d. How many whales explode each year.

_____ 2. What causes whales to explode?
  a. Drinking salt water.   **b.** Pressure from gases.
  c. Eating too much food.   **d.** Holes in their stomachs.

_____ 3. Which word or phrase from the reading means the same thing as "**pop**"?
  a. Burst.   **b.** Give up.   **c.** Act.   **d.** Save.

_____ 4. What does it mean when the reporter says, "**get to work**"?
  a. Throw cold water on the whale.
  b. Find some food for the whale.
  c. Cut holes in the whale's stomach.
  d. Call a doctor to come and help the whale.

_____ 5. What is "**a time bomb**"?
  a. A dangerous object.   **b.** A fun experience.
  c. A sad sight.   **d.** A funny story.

Movie Review

Movie Review

Wedding Day

Starring: Pete Barnes, Mary Fischer, Timothy Dale

Score: ★★★★☆

If you like **comedies**, you have to see this movie. Directed by

Michael Sharp (*Dream Girls, Police School*), this movie will have you

laughing non-stop for its full 120 minutes.

Josh Martin (Pete Barnes) is about to get married. But at the last

minute, he finds out that his future wife, Fey (Mary Fischer), is not

quite what she appears to be. Will he still marry her? Or will his wife's

secret be just too much for him?

The movie is full of jokes from start to finish, and Barnes gives a

great performance as the confused Josh. Also great is Timothy Dale.

He plays Josh's crazy best friend, Ralph. The scenes the two have

together are the funniest in the movie.

Though it doesn't quite get a full five stars (some scenes do take a

little too long), this movie still gets **a big thumbs-up** from me.

» clapboard

» audience

Questions

⌃ a big thumbs-up

_____ 1. What does the reading tell us?

   a. Someone's plans to make a new movie.

   b. How a movie changed someone's life.

   c. Someone's favorite movie of all time.

   d. Someone's thoughts about a movie he or she saw.

_____ 2. Who is not an actor in the movie?

   a. Pete Barnes.　　　　**b.** Michael Sharp.

   c. Timothy Dale.　　　　**d.** Mary Fischer.

_____ 3. How do you feel about something if you give it "a big thumbs-up"?

   a. You think it's perfect.　　**b.** You think it's too silly.

   c. You think it's very good.　**d.** You think it's too long.

_____ 4. What was most likely the writer's favorite thing about the movie?

   a. The scenes between Josh and Ralph.

   b. The ending.

   c. The character of Fey.

   d. The interesting story.

_____ 5. What kind of movie is a "comedy"?

   a. A funny movie.　　　　**b.** A scary movie.

   c. A sad movie.　　　　　**d.** A bloody movie.

46

Tears

Tears run down my face,
Leaving silver lines like snails
Moving through the grass,

Carrying heavy shells.
5 Tears run down my face; they run
Away like raindrops

On a window,
Taking the dark spots with them
As they fall and then

10 They disappear. Tears
Fall from my eyes like water
From a spring, which runs

Over sharp stones and
Through dark forests until,
15 After a time, it

Reaches a quiet sea.
Tears are the midday storm that
Clears the hot, gray air

And makes it fresh again,
20 Makes it possible to breathe
Again, to smile

Again. I am not afraid
Of tears; I welcome them.

⌃ raindrops

⌃ snail

⌃ storm

⌃ spring

Questions

_____ 1. What is the writer trying to say in the poem?

    a. It's difficult to focus when you're sad.

    b. Crying can make you feel better.

    c. Only weak people cry.

    d. Some people cry false tears.

_____ 2. What does the writer not compare tears to?

    a. Raindrops.   **b.** A storm.   **c.** Spring water.   **d.** The sea.

_____ 3. What is "**it**" in the poem?

    a. The writer's state of mind.   **b.** The writer's problem.

    c. The writer's tear.   **d.** The writer's smile.

_____ 4. How do you think the writer feels after crying?

    a. Angry.   **b.** Peaceful.   **c.** Scared.   **d.** Funny.

_____ 5. What does "**heavy shells**" mean in the poem?

    a. The writer's bags.   **b.** The writer's happy thoughts.

    c. The writer's troubles.   **d.** The writer's ideas.

47

(047)

An Interesting Way to Give a Gift

What is red, made of paper, and full of money? If you guessed a Chinese red envelope, you are right. But do you know **the customs behind giving and accepting such a gift**?

5   A red-colored envelope means something special. Red is a lucky color in Chinese culture. During Chinese New Year, younger generations get envelopes from parents and grandparents. Employees often get them from their bosses at this time, too. They are 10 also traditional wedding gifts. Sometimes people get red envelopes on their birthdays as well.

    The amount of money put inside the envelope is important. Only even amounts of money should be given. Odd numbers are bad luck. Also, it's important 15 not to give any amount of money with a four in it. The word for four in Mandarin sounds similar to the word for death! You should always give and accept red envelopes with both hands as a sign of respect.

⌃ Red is a lucky color in Chinese culture.

⌃ Younger generations get red envelopes from their elders.

Questions

_____ 1. What could be another name for this reading?
   a. Important Chinese Customs.   **b.** Spending Money in China.
   c. Different Types of Parties.   **d.** An Interesting Puzzle.

_____ 2. Why is it important not to give amounts of money with the number four in them?
   a. It's not enough money.   **b.** It's a funny number.
   c. It has a bad meaning.   **d.** It's a very important number.

_____ 3. What does "**the customs behind giving and accepting red envelopes**" mean in this reading?
   a. The reasons why people give and accept red envelopes in a certain way.
   b. The history of giving and accepting red envelopes.
   c. The special days when giving red envelopes is important.
   d. The different cultures in which people give red envelopes to each other.

_____ 4. Who is most likely to give a red envelope to someone?
   a. A baby.   **b.** A junior high school student.
   c. A grandparent.   **d.** A lucky person.

_____ 5. How should a person accept a red envelope from someone?
   a. By taking it with one hand.
   b. By asking him or her to put it on a table.
   c. By taking it with two hands.
   d. By not accepting it at first.

» Only even amounts of money should be put inside the envelope.

48 Who Works the Most Hours?

(048)

How many hours a year does the average American work? Are Americans lazier than workers from other countries? In fact, figures show that Americans work pretty hard compared to Europeans. But they still fall far behind workers in Asia.

⌃ The Germans now work the fewest hours per year.

5   Surprisingly, the Germans, who are often considered hard-working, now work the fewest hours per year. They even work fewer hours than the famously easygoing French!

So who are the world's hardest-working people? Well, **the crown** goes to the people of Hong Kong. The average worker

10   in Hong Kong works 2,400 hours per year! The Koreans, on

Questions

_____ 1. What does the reading compare about people from different countries?
  a. How rich they are.   **b.** How friendly they are.
  c. How hard-working they are.   **d.** How smart they are.

_____ 2. In the 1980s, who worked the most hours?
  a. The people of Hong Kong.   **b.** The Germans.
  c. The Koreans.   **d.** The Singaporeans.

_____ 3. What does "**the crown**" mean in the reading?
  a. The prize.   **b.** The king.
  c. The new job.   **d.** The top spot.

Average Hours Worked per Person per Year by Country

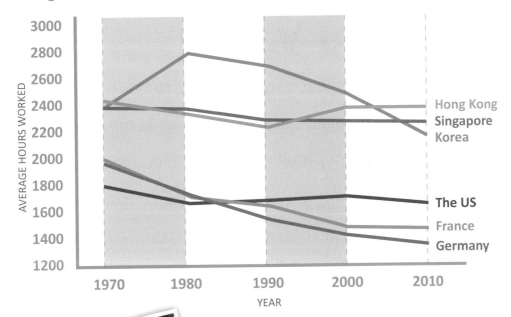

the other hand, seem to be taking things a little easier in recent years. They now only work an average of 2,200 hours a year, compared with a huge 2,800 in 1980.

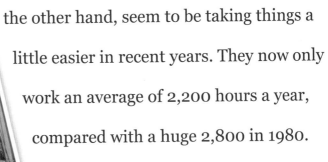

« Hong Kong people are the world's hardest-working people.

____ 4. What can't we know from the reading?

   a. Who worked the least hours per year in the 1990s.

   b. How many hours per year the French worked in 2000.

   c. Who worked the most hours per year in the 1960s.

   d. Who worked less than 1600 hours per year in 2010.

____ 5. What does the reading show?

   a. People in Asia like to take more days off than people in the West.

   b. In general, people in Asia work harder than people in the West.

   c. People in the West get sick more often than people in Asia.

   d. By 2020, people in the West will work more hours per year than Asians.

49 | Lake Valley

I love living in the city, but sometimes I like to get away from it all. So, this weekend I'm going to a beautiful spot out in the countryside called Lake Valley. There's a lake, and a forest, and some great mountain walks. I'm staying at a bed-and-breakfast in one of the little

5 villages nearby. I found out all about the area in this book called *Lake Valley and the Nearby Area*. The book has a great index, so it was easy to find everything I needed to know.

INDEX

A

accommodation 40-45
  bed-and-breakfasts
                42-44
  camping 45
  hotels 41
activities 20-27
  bicycle-riding 24
  bird-watching 21
  fishing 22
  sailing 23
  walking 25-27
animals, *see* nature
ATMs, *see* banks

B

banks 69
bed-and-breakfasts
                42-44
bicycle-riding 24
bird-watching 21
books
  local history 5
  nature guides 17
  walking guides 27
business hours 70

C

cafes 49
camping 45
car travel 73
children, traveling with
                55-56
churches 36
climate, *see* weather
clothing, *see* what to wear

» valley

» mountain walk

^ villages

Questions

_____ 1. What type of book does the index come from?

    a. A restaurant guide.   **b.** A nature guide.

    c. A guide to local history.   **d.** A travel guide.

_____ 2. I'm in Lake Valley and I need some cash. Which page of the book will tell me where there is an ATM?

    a. Page 69.   **b.** Page 45.   **c.** Page 73.   **d.** Page 5.

_____ 3. What is someone looking for if he or she searches for "**accommodation**" in the index?

    a. A place to stay.   **b.** A place to eat.

    c. A rare bird.   **d.** A famous sight.

_____ 4. On which page would you find these sentences?

Visiting Lake Valley with your kids can be a wonderful experience. There are plenty of fun things to do to keep them interested for days. There is even a local company, The Lake Valley Youth Club, which organizes special days out for kids aged between 7 and 12.

    a. Page 27.   **b.** Page 36.   **c.** Page 41.   **d.** Page 55.

_____ 5. What will I find on pages 25-27 of the book?

    a. The churches you can see in Lake Valley.

    b. The animals you can see in Lake Valley.

    c. The walks you can take in Lake Valley.

    d. The times shops open and close in Lake Valley.

50 Valentine's Day Set Menu

February 14 is Valentine's Day! Many couples celebrate their love by going out for a beautiful meal together, so on Valentine's Day restaurants are always full. Many restaurants also offer a special Valentine's Day menu. On the
5 right is an example of **one** from Mario's Italian Restaurant.

⌃ pizza

» spaghetti

⌃ chocolate cake

Questions

_____ **1.** Why is this menu special?
   a. A famous cook designed it.
   b. The dishes are all homemade.
   c. It's for one night only.
   d. Each meal comes with a free drink.

_____ **2.** I hate anything with tomato in it. Which of the following dishes shouldn't I order?
   a. Italian Wedding Soup.   **b.** Caesar Salad.
   c. Valentine's Kiss.   **d.** Spaghetti.

_____ **3.** What does "**one**" mean in the reading?
   a. A restaurant. **b.** A menu.   **c.** A course.   **d.** A dish.

Mario's Italian Restaurant
Valentine's Day Set Menu

Two Courses $20 / Three Courses $30

First Course

Caesar Salad
Fresh lettuce, cheese, lemon juice, and chicken

Or

Italian Wedding Soup
Chicken soup with green vegetables and meatballs

Main Course

Your Choice of Pizza (Heart-Shaped)
Four cheeses / Ham and pineapple / Cheese and tomato

Or

Spaghetti
Spaghetti with sauce made from tomato, beef, and onion

Dessert

Naughty-but-Nice Chocolate Cake
Dark chocolate cake with white chocolate sauce

Or

Valentine's Kiss
Cream pudding with strawberry sauce

Each meal includes a free soda, tea, or coffee.
We also add a 10% service charge to the final cost of the meal.

≫ Caesar salad

≪ Italian wedding soup

≪ cream pudding

4. For her main course, my girlfriend orders a pizza. Which of these is her pizza?

 **a.**   **b.**  **c.**  **d.**

5. My girlfriend had two courses, and I had three. What is the total cost of our meal?

   a. $55.   **b.** $50.   **c.** $60.   **d.** $66.

TRANSLATION

1 微笑的力量

你正在微笑嗎？什麼事能讓你微笑？也許當你見到朋友、吃到巧克力蛋糕或贏得大獎的時候會微笑。醫生認為我們應該笑口常開，因為有助於身心靈。當你微笑的時候：

• 你會感到開心
• 你能讓其他人感到開心
• 你看起來更漂亮
• 你可以不用言傳就讓人意會到你想表達的話語！

微笑是全世界共通的語言。6月15日甚至是所謂的「微笑力量日」，鼓勵大家在那天對陌生人微笑。但請小心！多數人能夠察覺真心微笑與假笑的差別。當你發自內心的微笑，你的嘴角和眼神都會充滿笑意；當你假笑的時候，你卻只會上揚嘴角。

何不試試看呢？真心地對你的老師微笑，看看老師是否也對你笑？

2 母親節卡片

給世上最偉大的媽媽：

　　妳是我夢寐以求最親切、最關心我、最棒的媽媽。

　　感謝妳總是照料我，感謝妳總是在我難過的時候替我打氣，還要感謝妳讓我總是無憂無慮！

　　我想讓妳知道，在我心中妳不只是媽媽而已，還是我的好朋友。所以我想在這個特別的節日，送上滿滿的愛與親親。

　　還有，我已經告訴老爸別再偷懶，讓妳放個假，他答應了。所以如果他沒有幫忙做家事，就等於食言而肥。希望他有將早餐送到妳床邊——我有提醒他喔。

愛妳喔。

妳可愛的女兒

珍

備註：希望妳喜歡我送的花，我知道妳最喜歡鬱金香！

3 寄宿體驗

親愛的淑芬：

　　妳好嗎？我在法國過得很開心！我的寄宿家庭是法國人，他們有個兒子叫麥可，女兒叫艾洛絲。我們幾乎天天都去海灘，因為天氣太熱了。只有週日會待在家，因為麥可和艾洛絲的祖父母會來拜訪。他們很親切，會帶糖果和漫畫書給我們。我試著和他們講法文，但法文實在很難。

　　明天我們要早起參觀一幢老城堡，麥可說那裡鬧鬼，但我不相信！我們參觀完會去一家知名的活魚餐廳吃晚餐，他們的漁獲都是早上現捕，採用燒烤的方式烹調。雖然法國料理的味道和台灣料理非常迥異，但我喜歡。

　　我想妳！下次聊。

美惠

4 長期使用 3C 產品易傷視力

醫師：哈囉，我能幫上什麼忙呢？

男子：我頭痛得不得了，不曉得為什麼。

醫師：你的飲食習慣怎麼樣？

男子：我只攝取健康飲食！所以不會有什麼問題。

醫師：好的，我可以檢查一下你的眼睛嗎？看起來很乾燥且充滿血絲。
　　　　你多久用一次電腦？

男子：每天，我是上班族。

醫師：你下班後通常有哪些活動？

男子：我用手機和朋友聊天，或去看電影。

醫師：所以你一整天都在用電腦，傍晚的時候仍然盯著螢幕！你當然會頭痛！

男子：我該怎麼辦？沒有網路我就沒辦法活了！

醫師：首先，確保你的螢幕亮度不能過亮。再來，每**20**分鐘要休息一下。最後，試著培養戶外嗜好，這樣也有助於你的整體健康狀態。

5 向朋友道歉

寄件人　tina_134@funmail.com

收件人　jenny1435@pcmailbox.com

日期　　2014年6月7日星期六　晚上9點

主旨　　對不起 :(

蒂娜：

　　我對所發生的事情感到很抱歉。艾咪叫我跟她一起逛街，我答應了。我知道她在學校說妳壞話之後，妳很討厭她，我當時真的沒想太多，妳是我最好的朋友，我保證以後不會再和她說話。我甚至覺得跟她出去不好玩，她一直都在聊自己的事，真的很無聊！

　　我可以做點什麼彌補妳嗎？我們明天出去吃冰淇淋好不好？去百貨公司裡妳很喜歡的那家店怎麼樣？我請客喔！這件事我真的很難過，蒂娜，希望妳能原諒我。

妳永遠的朋友

珍妮

6 與海豚共釣

　　巴西南端拉古納海域的海豚，會協助漁夫捕魚。海豚游來游去的時候，會把魚群推向靠近漁夫的海域。當魚群夠龐大時，海豚會以頭部或尾巴示意，讓漁夫知道何時該撒網。

　　此現象顯示，海豚屬於團結合作且能與人類共事的動物。也顯示出海豚十分聰明，因為牠們能無師自通。海豚知道幫助漁夫等於幫自己找到更多食物的道理。

　　科學家研究巴西的海豚已有兩年的時間，他們對此故事感興趣的原因在於不是每隻海豚都願意幫忙，這表示海豚和人類一樣：有的很熱心，有的則不盡然。

7 青少年的情緒健康

歡迎閱讀本書《你感覺如何？》

我們都知道，當一個青少年並不容易。老師交代太多功課；父母給的自由不夠多！三不五時還會和朋友、兄弟姐妹產生問題。有的時候你很開心且雀躍不已；有的時候又覺得傷心或生氣。

你已不再是小孩子，身心快速成長，讓你難以理解為何如此。好消息是：每個人都經歷過這樣的過程，你並非一人獨自面對。

本書會幫助你了解青春期的難題。書中第一部分，會說明你的情緒為何那麼容易快速轉變；第二部分則會教導你如何讓自己感覺更加正面！希望你喜歡閱讀本書。

8 打掃社區

麥克：你看那邊，有人就這樣把垃圾丟在人行道。

比爾：我知道。這個社區變得好髒亂。

麥克：我們應該想想辦法，讓大家多為這個社區的狀態著想。

比爾：好主意。我們來召開社區大會，就能和大家一起同時討論。

麥克：好，但是萬一大家不聽勸呢？

比爾：我們必須引起他們的注意。我知道了！接下來這幾天我們何不拍下地上遍布垃圾的照片？然後在大會上展示所有的照片。

麥克：好法子。這樣大家就能親眼瞧瞧問題有多嚴重。

比爾：是呀。或許我們還能呼朋引伴來打掃社區。

麥克：太好了。好，我們開始來邀請大家參加大會吧……

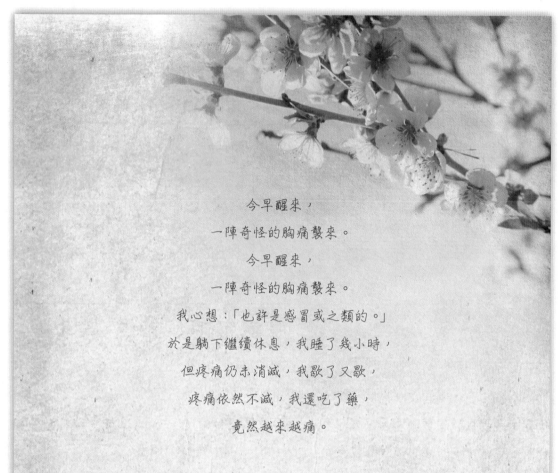

今早醒來，
一陣奇怪的胸痛襲來。
今早醒來，
一陣奇怪的胸痛襲來。
我心想：「也許是感冒或之類的。」
於是躺下繼續休息，我睡了幾小時，
但疼痛仍未消減，我歇了又歇，
疼痛依然不減，我還吃了藥，
竟然越來越痛。

我去看醫生，他說：「孩子，讓我診斷一下」；
我去看醫生，他說：「孩子，你沒有感冒。
你上次見到母親是什麼時候？
你得的是思鄉病。」

他說：「你需要的是母親做的家常菜，
嘗過以後就會痊癒。」
他說：「母愛是你的良藥，
見到她，你就會沒事。」

所以我準備返鄉看看母親，
她能驅散我的憂鬱鄉愁。

10 南瓜燈的製作方式

爸爸：好，我們開始動手吧。

珍妮：要先怎麼做呢？

爸爸：首先，拿這把麵包刀，小心地將南瓜頂端切開為蓋子狀。

珍妮：像這樣嗎？

爸爸：對，很好。

珍妮：接下來呢？

爸爸：現在我們以湯匙挖出裡面的瓜肉。

珍妮：我可以用手挖嗎？

爸爸：哈哈，妳喜歡的話當然可以。

珍妮：我們要丟掉裡面的瓜肉嗎？

爸爸：不，這樣太浪費。我們要把南瓜肉交給媽媽，她等一下可以拿來做成南瓜派！

珍妮：接下來呢？

爸爸：現在用這支筆，在南瓜外殼畫一張嚇人的臉孔。然後，我們會以刀子刻出臉孔的樣子。這個步驟有點麻煩，我來完成這個部分就好。

珍妮：現在我們只要放進蠟燭就好，對不對？

爸爸：沒錯。這樣妳就擁有一顆嚇人的南瓜燈囉！

11 誠徵室友

公告1：

有人需要室友嗎？

我是來自澳洲的塔拉，今年19歲，就讀歷史系。我很愛乾淨，能讓房間有條不紊，我也很親切！我希望擁有喜歡動物和愛看電影的室友。我正在學大提琴，所以有時候會在傍晚練習。如果你不介意琴聲吵，請打這支電話給我089-435-7139，或是傳送電子信箱至tarakeenan@knights.edu.au。

公告2：

我想找室友！

我叫海倫，來自美國。我想找18歲至20歲、會講英文的女生室友。我希望室友的個性文靜，能讓房間有條不紊。我喜愛貓和狗狗、畫畫與打棒球，而且我很早起。如果妳覺得ok，我們何不一起住？請打這支電話給我089-237-2894，或傳送電子信箱至htyo@gmail.com。

12 別狼吞虎嚥

男子：我們今晚要去那家新餐廳嗎？

女子：跟你去餐廳吃飯沒意思，你總是吃得很快！

男子：那又怎麼樣？吃東西是一種享受。

女子：我也很享受！所以我會從容的吃。在10分鐘內吃完飯，怎麼可能好好品嚐食物呢？

男子：如果吃太久，食物就會涼掉。

女子：但是你這樣不會胃痛嗎？

男子：不會。

女子：依我之見，吃飯應該是件愉悅的事。一邊慢慢吃、一邊聊天才有意思。

男子：我們可以在飯前和飯後聊天呀。我真搞不懂妳，妳今晚到底要不要和我吃晚餐？

女子：喔，我會跟你去……前提是你答應我不能狼吞虎嚥，拜託就這麼一次！

13 盲貓荷馬的冒險旅程

發文時間：2013年8月22日下午4點12分

再會了，荷馬

　　本部落格的讀者，一定知道我有多愛貓！今天我很傷心，因為其中一隻全球最知名的貓去世了，那就是享年11歲的「神奇盲貓」—— 荷馬。

　　荷馬的主人葛雯・庫柏在網上分享他的故事，許多國家的讀者都想一窺荷馬的經歷。葛雯描述荷馬雖然眼盲，卻是一隻十分勇敢的貓咪。某晚，有名男子闖入葛雯的家，荷馬攻擊這名歹徒而救了葛雯。2009年，她出版荷馬的故事，用意在於為其他動物籌募善款。

　　人們因為荷馬的緣故，改變了對盲貓的看法。以往貓咪如果天生眼盲，獸醫都束手無策。現在，大家知道眼盲的動物仍能擁有不錯的生活品質。

　　再會了，荷馬，也謝謝你，一路好走。

珍妮：妳有跟克里斯聊到我嗎？

凱特：有啊。

珍妮：天啊，我好緊張！他怎麼說？他有說他喜歡我嗎？

凱特：這個嘛，他是有說喜歡妳⋯⋯

珍妮：什麼？真的假的？天啊！我太開心了！

凱特：等等，珍妮。妳先別太興奮。雖然他說喜歡妳，但不是妳想的那樣。

珍妮：等等⋯⋯什麼？什麼意思？

凱特：意思是他把妳當朋友般的喜歡，僅此而已。我很抱歉，我知道妳很迷戀他。我猜他對妳沒有感覺。

珍妮：好吧，但等等，他確切的用字是什麼？

凱特：我問他：「你有女朋友嗎？」他說沒有。我又說：「你覺得珍妮怎麼樣？」他說：「我覺得她人很好，但是她不是我喜歡的類型。」

15 音樂電台廣播

♪♪喔，音樂讓我會心一笑，絕對是最佳的療癒良藥♪♪

《療癒良藥》是愛德安‧威廉斯的歌曲。很棒的一首歌，獻給來自新橋的麥克。歡迎大家收聽，如果你才剛轉到這台，這裡是《早餐秀》，我是主持人克里斯安‧歐布萊恩。今天我們要開放點歌，請傳簡訊至 **877-543**，告訴我們你最喜歡的歌曲，我會盡我所能地在節目開始和結束前播放你點的歌。稍後要播放的是「百萬姐妹」的《時間到》，之後則會播放「賽門雙子星」的《別煩我》。不過現在我要先撥放「週五女孩」的《整夜狂歡》，這首歌獻給來自奧克戴爾的派特，希望你喜歡。一起來欣賞「週五女孩」的《整夜狂歡》。

♪♪週五之夜到來了，喔耶！週五之夜到來了，喔耶！♪♪

16 泰國潑水節

在我的祖國泰國，我們最重視的節慶就是潑水節。潑水節等同我們的新年，時間都在四月，十分熱鬧有趣。此慶典眾所皆知，因為可以任意向他人潑水！而其目的則在於為明年帶來好運。此外，你還能在路邊攤買到美味的食物，例如佐以特殊醬料的木瓜或雞肉。

很多人會在潑水節返鄉與家人團聚。節慶第一天，會進行居家大掃除；第二天開始潑水慶典；第三天則會前往廟宇朝拜並清洗佛像，清洗用的水有浸泡過花朵，佛像因而散發出清香。潑水節算是我一年中最喜歡的節日。

17 尷尬的一刻

　　那天是黛安上學的第一天，她很擔心沒有人喜歡她。第一堂課是英文課，老師是史密斯先生，他要所有的學生兩兩一組完成指定作業。班上所有同學很快就找到搭檔，只有黛安沒有伴，所以史密斯先生主動說要和黛安一組，有的同學開始笑，讓黛安很想找地方躲起來。

　　午餐的時候，有個親切的女孩叫做安，她問黛安要不要和她與其他朋友一起吃飯。她還關心黛安，第一天上學過得怎麼樣。黛安回應：「還可以，但我不喜歡我的英文老師，他要和我搭檔做作業，他好奇怪！」

　　此時全桌同學鴉雀無聲，黛安不曉得自己說錯了什麼。最後，安的朋友蒂娜說：「史密斯先生是安的父親。」黛安頓時真想撞牆。

18 公車時刻表

　　今天是週六，適逢夏季時節，而且氣候宜人。我和朋友們準備前往白沙灣一日遊，享受陽光、沙灘與海洋！我們最好加快腳步，否則會錯過公車！

蓋瑞市—白沙灣		2015年夏季　5月1日－9月30日				
		週一至週五		週六/週日/國定假日		
停靠站		時間	時間	時間	時間	時間
蓋瑞市 (公車站)	起站	8:30	10:30	8:30	9:30	10:30
蓋瑞市 (長街)		8:35	10:35	8:35	9:35	10:35
蓋瑞市 (史帝芬街)		8:40	10:40	8:40	9:40	10:40
城堡鎮		8:55	10:55	8:55	9:55	10:55
歐克戴爾		9:10	11:10	9:10	10:10	11:10
清水		9:20	11:20	9:20	10:20	11:20
舊橋		9:35	11:35	9:35	10:35	11:35
新港		9:45	11:45	9:45	10:45	11:45
白沙灣	到站	9:48	11:48	9:48	10:48	11:48
票價：蓋瑞市至白沙灣　單程票：7元　　來回票：12元 *乘客可於車上或蓋瑞市公車站購票處購買車票。						

19 自然就是美

　　每每翻開雜誌，我們都會看見穿著高檔服飾的俊男美女照片，也會想要打扮得和這些雜誌人物一樣。我們很容易被說服，只要買下那樣的服飾就能讓自己開心，但是這樣的造型風格適合自己嗎？

　　衣著代表我們的形象，所以請慎選服裝！聖羅蘭品牌的服裝師曾說道：「時尚趨勢來來去去，只有有型才能長久。」他的意思是人比衣裝更重要。當你能自在接受真實的自己時，再怎麼樣都很有型。

　　如果你的牛仔褲價值不斐，你就會擔心果汁潑灑在褲子上。如果你的鞋子咬腳，你一整天都會心情抑鬱。你的打扮流行與否並不重要，因為神采飛揚的氣質必須由內而外散發出來，所以只要選擇讓你心情愉快的服飾即可。

彼特：嘿，傑克，我需要你的幫忙。

傑克：好啊，彼特。怎麼了？

彼特：我問凱薩琳願不願意和我出去約會，她答應了。我這週六想帶她去吃晚餐。

傑克：太好了！那你為什麼需要我的幫忙？

彼特：問題是，我很不會約會，我不想搞砸這次的經驗。

傑克：你需要小撇步嗎？

彼特：沒錯。

傑克：這樣吧，我借你我的約會大全。

彼特：那是什麼？

傑克：這本書超酷，能教你一些約會技巧。

彼特：太感謝了，老兄，你真是太棒了。

感謝您於shoes4u.com購物，希望您喜歡所購買的新鞋！不過，若您對訂單有任何疑問，請與我們聯絡。我們將盡快處理問題。

購物常見問題：

Q: 我已經下訂單，卻沒收到鞋子。

A: 請傳送電子郵件至help@shoes4u.com，並告知您的姓名與訂單編號，我們將重新寄出一雙鞋款。

Q: 我訂錯尺寸。

A: 請於14天內退貨即可，我們將寄出正確尺寸的鞋款。
退貨地址列於本頁最下方。

Q: 我改變主意，希望能退款。

A: 抱歉，我們無法退款！但您可從我們的網站選購不同鞋款。

如有其他任何疑問，請撥打080-465-0099，將有專員樂於為您服務。

---

22 用右手？還是左手？

阿吉特：謝謝妳來看我，瑪麗。

瑪麗：不不，我才該謝謝你邀請我來，我真不敢相信自己終於來印度觀光了。

阿吉特：下飛機後一定很餓吧，我們去吃東西。

瑪麗：太好了。你知道我很愛吃印度料理。

不久之後

瑪麗：好好吃！味道真棒。

阿吉特：等一下，瑪麗。

瑪麗：怎麼了？

阿吉特：妳用左手吃飯。

瑪麗：是啊。有什麼不妥嗎？

阿吉特：是這樣的，我們在印度不用左手吃飯。

瑪麗：為什麼？

阿吉特：因為這裡的人通常上完廁所後，是用左手擦屁股。

瑪麗：喔，我懂了。所以用右手會比較禮貌。

阿吉特：沒錯。

瑪麗：那我猜用左手拿東西給人家也很無禮囉？

阿吉特：哈哈！是的，妳學得很快嘛。

23 仲夏之夜

仲夏之夜

仲夏之夜——太陽逐漸西下；

漫長的夏日裡，我等待著你。

最後的光芒，就這麼消逝、消逝著，

但我的腦海裡，都是難忘的你。

夜風微拂，輕放

我捨不得結束的夏季之歌。

仲夏之夜——太陽逐漸西下；

漫長的夏日裡，我等待著你。

明月高掛夜空，皎潔又帶灰調，

取代了曾在同處綻放光芒的太陽。

我的記憶如同月亮陰晴圓缺，而我的希望，

逐漸消耗殆盡。

我的太陽啊，你已遠去，孤單的我卻須留下。

仲夏之夜——太陽逐漸西下；

漫長的夏日裡，我等待著你。

24 異物哽噎急救法

我上週參加了急救課程，學到如何幫助有難之人的方法。其中一項就是如何協助噎到的人。我們老師發了一張實用的講義，有助於我們記得步驟。以下是講義內容：

哽噎急救法

哽噎的可能情況：

- 患者無法呼吸、咳嗽或講話。
- 患者以雙手示意「我噎著了」的樣子
- 患者嘴唇發紫。

步驟 1 詢問「你噎到了嗎？」
步驟 2 如果患者示意回應「是的」，請站在他／她的後方，
　　　　將你的雙手環繞於他／她的腰部。
步驟 3 雙手手掌互扣，並放於此人的肚臍正上方。
步驟 4 往你自己的方向用力擠按患者。
步驟 5 重複動作，直到患者吐出異物或可呼吸為止。

25 奇特的動物：雙髻鯊

雙髻鯊猶如一海底謎團。牠的頭型為什麼會像一隻槌子？答案尚無人知曉。多年來，大家都以為雙髻鯊的頭型有助於嗅聞食物，或加快游速。但如今，我們對此奇特動物有了新的見解。

雙髻鯊的視力似乎因為這樣的頭型而優於其他鯊魚。雖然眼距極寬，卻能上下左右觀望，還能直視前方。因此可輕易推測自己和其他魚類之間的距離，這代表著雙髻鯊可輕易地獵捕食物。

雙髻鯊的臉型經歷過數千年的演變。隨著臉部面積增大，更能清楚看見周遭海域的情況，捕獲更多的魚類進食，也因此雙髻鯊的演變原因其實是來自於生存本能。

26 吉姆的行事曆

嗨，我是吉姆，生活十分忙碌。我勤奮工作，也喜歡從事許多有趣的活動，所以我使用月曆來記錄自己的行程內容和時間。請看一下我今年三月的行事曆。

三月

週一	週二	週三	週四	週五	週六	週日
1	2	3	4 公司重大會議（準備簡報）	5	6 老媽的生日（寄卡片）	7 下午4點去珍妮家烤肉
8	9	10 晚上9點和大顆兒去「月光」喝幾杯	11 和珍妮看電影	12	13	14 早上11點和麥克一起吃早午餐
15	16 晚上7點的每月讀書會		19 休假（打包度假的行李）	20 早上8:30飛往巴黎	21
22	23 從巴黎回來	24 開始上班	25 晚上7:30和老爸在「馬力歐餐廳」吃晚餐	26	27 藝術展（最後一天）	28 瑪麗的喜酒（買禮物）
29	30	31				

朵莉絲專欄　每週一刊載

朵莉絲負責解決青少年的煩惱！

親愛的朵莉絲：

我有個大問題。

　　我的好友對我態度冷淡，她不肯和我說話，打電話給她也不接。在學校時，只要我試著和她說話，她就走開。奇怪的是，我根本不知道她為什麼會這樣！我覺得自己並沒有做什麼事惹怒她。

我該怎麼辦？

疑惑女孩，17歲，來自台北

親愛的疑惑女孩：

　　或許她並不是氣妳做過什麼事，而是在氣妳沒有做的事。也許妳忘了送她生日禮物或關心她約會順不順利。有時是我們沒做的事惹惱了別人。她或許覺得被忽略，所以也想讓妳體會一下相同的感受。讓妳的朋友知道妳關心她，她很快就會忘掉這一切。

朵莉絲

---

28 流行樂巨星專訪

■ **您何時開始作曲？為什麼想作曲呢？**

大概是十歲的時候。我不太確定原因，自然而然就開始創作了。

■ **成為知名流行樂巨星的感覺如何？**

我很喜歡以作曲和音樂表演維生，但另一方面，我卻沒有私生活！

■ **您最引以為傲的歌曲是哪一首？**

我想我最引以為傲的是《多愛我一點》——這是我的第一首熱門金曲，花了我不少時間修潤，但儘管過了多年，我還是對成果很滿意。

■ **您會給想要成為藝人的人哪些建議？**

確保大家聽到你的音樂，網路是很好的宣傳媒介。畢竟，我也是從上傳歌曲至YouTube起家。現在，我已有機會為許多人演出我的歌曲。

29 校園霸凌

2015年3月17日星期二

親愛的日記：

　　我今天很衰，吉米・湯普森和他的朋友在午餐時間又找我麻煩。他不斷辱罵我，我試著遠離現場，他卻抓住我，將我推倒在地，然後開始嘲笑我。幸好有老師經過，事情才沒有越演越烈，吉米還假裝扶我起來，推說是我自己跌倒，背地裡跟我說他明天會繼續欺負我。現在我很怕上學，我應該請病假嗎？不行，吉米會知道我怕他，這樣他就稱心如意了，我必須勇敢起來，如果我讓他覺得他的所作所為不會影響到我，也許他就會收手。反正值得一試，我會讓你知道明天的發展，祝我好運吧⋯⋯

30 柏克萊科學博物館

　　我朋友和我預計在本週末參觀科學博物館，我們本來不太確定如何抵達，因此查看了博物館網站上的交通資訊。

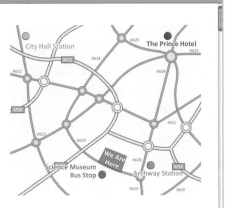

柏克萊科學博物館(我們的位置)

搭乘地鐵：

綠線　於拱門站下站。僅需步行五分鐘即可抵達博物館。

橘線　在市政廳站下站，搭乘42B號、236號或53號公車抵達柏克萊科學博物館。公車會在博物館入口處停靠。

自行開車：

南下：走M38南下道路，左轉至M32，再左轉至A624，博物館在您的左側。

北上：走M32北上道路，右轉至A624，博物館在您的左側。

搭乘公車：

由柏克萊西側公車站(53號、21號、34號)、市政廳地鐵站(42B號、236號、53號)以及王子飯店(21號、34號)所出發的公車均可抵達柏克萊科博物館。如需下載完整的公車時刻表，請點選這裡。

31 狗狗看得見顏色嗎？

傑夫‧詹姆斯撰文

　　很多人認為狗狗只看得見黑色和白色，但事實並非如此。科學家近期發現狗狗看得見顏色，只是和我們認知的顏色不同。

　　當我們看見彩虹時，看到的是紫色、藍色、靛青色、綠色、黃色、橙色、紅色。但當狗狗看見彩虹時，牠看到的是灰色、藍色、灰色、黃褐色、黃色與黃褐色，你能想像嗎？

　　狗狗將紅色和綠色視為同樣的顏色（黃褐色），將靛青色和紫色視為同樣的顏色（灰色）。這代表了如果你幫狗狗買了一個鮮紅色的玩具，牠看到的會是醜醜的黃褐色。

　　這原理是什麼呢？因為人類眼睛以三種不同的細胞組成來感應色彩，狗狗卻只有兩種細胞，因此狗狗的眼睛能看見的色彩範圍有限。

32 職缺資訊

徵才啟事

皮爾餐廳是市中心以出色法式料理聞名的熱門法國餐廳，我們以自己優質的料理與服務為傲。現在，我們徵求兩名新人加入我們的團隊。

職位：**廚師**(全職)

求職條件：
- 擁有在優良餐廳擔任廚師至少四年的經驗
- 熟稔法式料理與烹調技巧
- 願意長時間工作
- 喜歡團體作業

待遇：
- 每月30,000－40,000元台幣
- 週休兩天

職位：**男/女服務生** (週末兼職)

求職條件：
- 待人親切
- 勤勉工作
- 肯學習

不需工作經驗

待遇：
- 起薪每小時130元台幣

如有應徵意願，請將您的履歷傳送至 pierre@webmail.com.tw。

33 享受大自然

　　都市地區總是喧囂擁擠，你會聽見喇叭和垃圾車經過的聲音；公車上的吵雜對話聲與嬰兒哭聲。入夜後，到處看得見車輛、商店、餐廳與公寓大樓的燈光。你是否曾想遠離這一切？

　　如果你追求的是平靜安詳的感覺，非常簡單，何不到森林野餐和健行？如果附近有海灘，何不脫下鞋子，踩沙散步？都市環境裡同樣也能看見大自然的蹤影，多數都市均設有充滿綠地、樹林和花圃的公園，你甚至可以帶本書，坐在公園長凳上閱讀。

　　即使你非常忙碌，還是能撥冗駐足聞聞玫瑰花香。享受大自然的機會唾手可得，最棒的是完全免費！

34 跳蚤市場廣告海報

二手服飾		家常菜
CD 與 DVD 光碟	本週六舉辦 跳蚤市場活動	
藝術品	請至以下網站登記賣家身分 www.hanovermarket.com 每桌費用5元 開賣時間：9:00-13:00 13:00-17:00	二手書

本週六（5月9日）的早上9點至下午5點，將於小鎮廣場舉辦跳蚤市場。歡迎大家前來！如欲出售物品，可上網登記賣家身份，或前來逛逛，瞧瞧是否有任何物品吸引你的目光！

你是畫家嗎？何不來販售你的畫作？

你是烘培師傅嗎？何不來販售你的蛋糕？

你想清空自己的眾多雜物嗎？

你的無用之物或許是別人眼中的珍寶！

歡迎前來一探究竟，度過開心的一天！

買家免費入場！

35 籃球

裝水蜜桃的籃子和足球有何共通點？你猜得出來答案是「籃球」嗎？籃球運動起源於 **1891** 年，該運動的發明者是位名叫約翰・奈史密斯的加拿大人，目的是讓運動員於漫長的冬季時節，仍能在室內保持活躍體能。

多年來，籃球運動的形式演變許多，水蜜桃籃被中空的籃圈取代，讓賽事節奏更緊湊，因為無須暫停取出籃中的籃球。早期的籃球運動使用的是足球，爾後才出現專為此運動所設計的特殊球體。

十九世紀晚期，籃球運動流傳於加拿大和美國，高中與大專院校均教授此熱門運動。如今，全球皆風行籃球運動，可說是史上最熱門的運動之一。

36 亨利八世

亨利八世是英格蘭享譽盛名的國王之一。他不僅為強勢的軍事領導統帥，更是才華洋溢的詩人與音樂家。不過，他最為家喻戶曉的事蹟還是他的六段婚姻。以下是他的亨利精彩的情史年表。

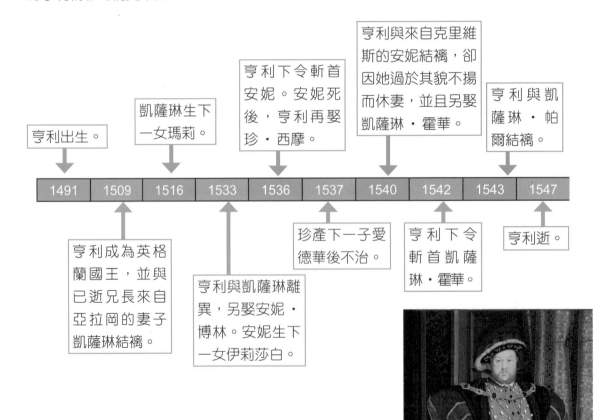

37 打工度假簽證

大洋洲 打工度假簽證

享受畢生美好的時光

每年都有許多年輕人申請前往大洋洲打工度假的簽證。

拿到打工度假簽證後你可以：

- 於大洋洲自由旅行一年。
- 隨時藉由打工的方式補助自己的旅費。
- 就學長達六個月的時間。

只有**18歲**至**30歲**的青年可申請打工度假簽證。

如需了解打工度假簽證方面的更多資訊與申請方式，請至 WWW.OCEANIA.GOV.OC

> 我過得好開心。唯一美中不足的就是最後得回家了！
>
> 喬，27歲，來自倫敦

> 一定要體驗！絕對會改變你的一生！實在像一場超棒的冒險！
>
> 麥克，22歲，來自台北

> 我認識好多有趣的人，還結交不少新朋友。
>
> 蓋兒，25歲，來自紐約

38 聰明理財術

智慧瓦力每日部落格

本週每日金玉良言
智慧瓦力教你聰明理財的大絕招

2015年4月19日，由智慧瓦力發文

哈囉，讀者們！我們都知道賺錢不易，因此我列出能讓大家財源滾滾的方法。

1. 多花一點錢。

別擔心多為優質的物品多花一點錢，因為便宜商品容易磨損或故障，多花一點錢，長遠來看反而是省錢。

2. 等待特賣時機。

你現在真的即刻需要購入新的夏季洋裝嗎？可以等到秋季，就能以半價買到，明年夏天一樣可以穿。

3. 買二手貨。

現在很流行二手店與二手市場，你可以從中挑選到很不錯的玩意兒，例如教科書、衣服、DVD光碟等應有盡有，你所挖到的寶絕對會讓你驚喜連連。

39 遛狗服務

遛狗服務

您忙到沒有時間遛狗嗎？
交給我們準沒錯！

你知道多數狗狗每天需要運動 30 到 60 分鐘，來維持身心健康嗎？然而倘若您有全職工作或小孩，可能很難騰出這麼多空閒時間。

交給我們就對了！

我們的遛狗團隊能確保您的愛犬獲得充分的運動量，還能讓狗狗樂在其中！

您可安排一般遛狗時段，或於緊急情況下臨時通知我們，我們能在兩個小時內趕到幫您遛狗。

下次您忠實的狗狗需要運動時，記得撥個電話通知我們！

- 一般服務：每小時 10 元
- 緊急服務 (於 12 小時內通知)：每小時 15 元

40 電玩遊戲真的有害嗎？

年輕人都愛玩電玩遊戲，這是不爭的事實。另一個現實情況是，年輕人有時會有不法舉動，只要他們行為乖張，例如重傷他人，大家就會想要歸咎原因。在過去人們會怪罪卡通、動作片，甚至是搖滾樂，現在則是將矛頭指向電玩遊戲。

但是玩電玩遊戲真的會讓人行為不當嗎？近期的研究結果似乎認同這樣的說法。首先，科學家要求一組學生玩電玩遊戲，有些人扮演英雄的角色；有些人扮演壞人的角色。之後，科學家要求學生們見到陌生人時，自行選擇獎勵或懲罰的作為。曾扮演「英雄」角色的學生偏好選擇獎勵陌生人 (送出巧克力)；但曾扮演「壞人」的學生則偏好懲罰陌生人 (讓陌生人吃辣椒醬)。此研究顯示，即使玩一下電玩遊戲，也會改變你在現實生活裡待人接物的模式。

41 聖代食譜

　　我的朋友們待會兒要來家裡聚會，我們要看電影、聊天，還有吃一大堆冰淇淋。其實，我想幫他們做我最喜歡的甜點：巧克力香蕉聖代。超好吃的，而且做法簡單快速，不一會兒功夫即可完成。食譜如下，你也可以幫你的朋友準備！

巧克力香蕉聖代食譜

4人份/製作時間：5分鐘

食材
- 小香蕉4條
- 1桶香草冰淇淋
- 1瓶巧克力醬
- 1/4杯巧克力米

做法
步驟1：香蕉去皮。
步驟2：將香蕉切成圓片狀。
步驟3：將冰淇淋均分至四個碗。

步驟4：將香蕉片鋪於冰淇淋上。
步驟5：將巧克力醬淋在冰淇淋和香蕉片上。
步驟6：再將巧克力米撒在上面。
步驟7：拿起湯匙開始享用！

42 與家人出國旅遊

　　我剛結束生平第一次出國旅遊的體驗——在英國玩一整個禮拜！我和爸媽、兩個兄弟和溫妮阿姨一起去。我們頭幾天先待在倫敦，跑遍所有景點，還參觀了一些很棒的博物館，我們甚至去參觀了英國女王的官邸白金漢宮！

　　然後我們從倫敦出發，搭火車一路前往蘇格蘭的愛丁堡。無庸置疑，愛丁堡最棒的特色就是城堡，溫妮阿姨在城堡前拍了超多照片，我們還在愛丁堡吃了哈吉斯，哈吉斯是一道以羊胃袋塞入羊心、羊肝與羊肺的料理！也許聽起來有點可怕，但味道還不賴。我的家人和我在旅途期間玩得十分盡興，我等不及下次出國玩的機會！

43 閱讀的好處

　　我所謂的「閱讀」，指的並不是快速瀏覽部落格內容或是讀取簡訊，大家應該都看得出來，這種讀取方式和真正浸淫在好書世界裡的「閱讀」有著天壤之別。我所謂的閱讀具有許多益處。當你看書的時候，你會將注意力放在故事情節，這樣做能減壓與增進自己的專注力和記憶力。現在思考一下你閱讀網路文章的感覺，你當下的注意力或許在文章上，但很快就會開始看信箱、對著好笑的圖片大笑，或是觀賞貓咪影片，你的心思放在很多地方。試著每天至少花上 15～20 分鐘靜靜的看書，你會對於閱讀改變生活這件事感到驚訝不已。

44 鯨魚為什麼會爆炸？

加拿大南岸有隻瀕死鯨魚擱淺。

經過數小時的拯救，救援小組已放棄希望。

但是該小組即將面臨新的問題。

因為鯨魚一旦死亡，形同定時炸彈。

鯨魚屍體開始腐壞後，體內會積聚氣體。

救援小組必須想辦法洩出氣體，否則鯨魚就會爆炸！

2012 年的愛爾蘭影片顯示處理欲爆炸鯨魚的方法。

當地人在海灘發現這隻死鯨魚，而且體內早已充滿危險的氣體。

這隻鯨魚隨時都可能爆炸，因此救援小組的動作十分迅速。

他們在鯨魚的屍體上切割出上百個小孔。

這些小孔能逐漸降低屍體內的壓力。

再回頭看加拿大的案例，這隻鯨魚已死亡，因此救援小組必須趕緊處置。

《大喜之日》

演員卡司：彼得・巴恩斯、瑪麗・費雪、提摩西・戴爾

評分：★★★★☆

　　如果你喜歡喜劇，一定要看這部電影。由麥克・夏普執導(作品有《夢幻女郎》、《警校物語》)，片長120分鐘，讓你一路笑到底。

　　喬許・馬丁(彼得・巴恩斯飾演)即將步入婚姻，但是在最後一刻，他發現老婆菲(瑪麗・費雪飾演)的身分另有隱情。他仍會娶她嗎？還是老婆的秘密會令他難以招架？

　　本片從開場到結尾笑點不斷，恩斯更將一頭霧水的喬許扮演得維妙維肖。提摩西・戴爾的表現同樣出色，他飾演喬許的瘋狂好友勞夫，只要有兩位同台演出的畫面，就是本片最爆笑的橋段。

　　雖然本片並未獲得五顆星的評價——某些橋段有點拖戲——但對我來說還是值得按讚。

淚水劃過我的臉龐，
彷彿蝸牛，
走過草地所留下的銀亮痕跡，

揹著沉重的殼。
淚水劃過我的臉龐，
彷彿打在窗戶的雨水，

落下時將窗戶上的汙點，
一起帶走消逝。

我眼眶泛出的淚水，
彷彿奔湧於銳石和黑暗森林的泉水，
直到一段時間後，

流入沉靜的海洋。
淚水宛如午後雷陣雨，
淨空悶熱灰暗的空氣，

讓空氣再度清新，
令人能再次呼吸。

再次微笑，
我並不怕淚水，
我欣然迎接它的到來。

47 有趣的贈禮方式

外觀為紅色紙袋又能裝錢的物品是什麼呢？如果你猜中國紅包，完全正確。但你知道施受紅包的習俗怎麼來的嗎？

紅包具有特殊意義，以中國文化而言，紅色是幸運色，中國新年期間，晚輩會收到父母與祖父母給的紅包；員工同樣會在過年拿到老闆發放的紅包。紅包更是傳統的喜酒禮金，有時生日的時候也會收到紅包。

紅包裡的金額十分重要，僅能放入偶數金額，奇數代表厄運。此外，重點在於金額數字裡不能有「四」，因為中文的「四」諧音近似「死」！還有，應雙手送出與收受紅包以示敬意。

48 哪國人的工時最長？

美國人一年的平均工時有多長呢？美國人是否比其他國家的勞工還要偷懶呢？事實上，數據顯示與歐洲人相較，美國人十分勤奮工作，但仍不及亞洲勞工。

令人驚訝的是，常給人刻苦工作印象的德國人，全年工時竟然最少，甚至比悠閒出名的法國人還要少！

那麼誰才是全球最吃苦耐勞的勞工呢？奪冠的是香港人。香港勞工的全年平均工時為 2400 小時！另一方面，韓國人似乎近年來開始放慢步調，與 1980 年代驚人的 2800 小時相較下，韓國人現在的全年平均工時為 2200 小時。

　　我喜歡居住於都市，但有時會想遠離塵囂。所以，我將於這個週末前往郊外一個叫做「湖谷」的美麗景點，可欣賞到湖泊、森林以及登山步道。我會住在附近小村莊的民宿，我是在《湖谷與週遭景點》的這本書瞭解此處，本書的索引設計很棒，因此可以輕鬆查找我需要知道的資訊。

2月14日是情人節！許多夫妻（情侶）都會在這一天外出享用大餐來慶祝愛情。因此，情人節時的各家餐廳皆門庭若市，很多餐廳還會特別推出情人節菜單，馬力歐義大利餐廳的菜單就是其中一個例子。

馬力歐義大利餐廳

情人節套餐菜單

兩道菜 $20　三道菜 $30

開胃菜
凱薩沙拉
新鮮萵苣、起司、檸檬汁與雞肉

或

義式風味湯
雞湯搭配綠色蔬菜和肉丸

主菜
任選披薩（心型）
四種起司口味 / 火腿鳳梨口味 /
起司番茄口味

或

義大利麵
義大利麵佐番茄牛肉洋蔥肉醬

甜點
淘氣甜蜜巧克力蛋糕
黑巧克力佐白巧克力醬

或

情人之吻
奶油布蕾佐草莓醬

每份餐點均附免費汽水、茶飲或咖啡結帳時
需另計10％服務費

ANSWERS

1	1. c	2. b	3. c	4. a	5. d
2	1. c	2. d	3. c	4. b	5. d
3	1. c	2. a	3. c	4. b	5. a
4	1. c	2. a	3. b	4. c	5. a
5	1. a	2. c	3. b	4. a	5. a

6	1. d	2. b	3. a	4. c	5. a
7	1. d	2. c	3. d	4. a	5. b
8	1. c	2. a	3. c	4. c	5. b
9	1. c	2. a	3. d	4. c	5. c
10	1. b	2. c	3. a	4. c	5. c

11	1. b	2. c	3. c	4. a	5. c
12	1. d	2. a	3. b	4. b	5. b
13	1. c	2. c	3. a	4. d	5. b
14	1. b	2. c	3. c	4. a	5. d
15	1. b	2. d	3. c	4. a	5. c

16	1. d	2. b	3. a	4. a	5. b
17	1. a	2. c	3. c	4. d	5. b
18	1. c	2. b	3. c	4. a	5. b
19	1. c	2. a	3. b	4. d	5. b
20	1. a	2. c	3. c	4. b	5. a

21	1. d	2. b	3. a	4. a	5. d
22	1. b	2. b	3. c	4. b	5. d
23	1. d	2. d	3. d	4. b	5. a
24	1. c	2. b	3. c	4. c	5. a
25	1. d	2. b	3. d	4. c	5. c

26	**1.** d	**2.** a	**3.** b	**4.** c	**5.** a
27	**1.** c	**2.** b	**3.** d	**4.** a	**5.** c
28	**1.** a	**2.** c	**3.** b	**4.** c	**5.** d
29	**1.** b	**2.** c	**3.** a	**4.** c	**5.** a
30	**1.** c	**2.** d	**3.** c	**4.** a	**5.** d

31	**1.** b	**2.** a	**3.** c	**4.** b	**5.** c
32	**1.** c	**2.** c	**3.** c	**4.** c	**5.** b
33	**1.** a	**2.** c	**3.** b	**4.** a	**5.** d
34	**1.** b	**2.** c	**3.** c	**4.** a	**5.** b
35	**1.** b	**2.** b	**3.** d	**4.** b	**5.** d

36	**1.** c	**2.** b	**3.** c	**4.** a	**5.** d
37	**1.** a	**2.** c	**3.** b	**4.** d	**5.** c
38	**1.** b	**2.** b	**3.** c	**4.** d	**5.** a
39	**1.** c	**2.** a	**3.** b	**4.** b	**5.** a
40	**1.** b	**2.** c	**3.** d	**4.** a	**5.** c

41	**1.** a	**2.** a	**3.** b	**4.** c	**5.** a
42	**1.** a	**2.** c	**3.** a	**4.** b	**5.** d
43	**1.** d	**2.** a	**3.** c	**4.** b	**5.** a
44	**1.** a	**2.** b	**3.** a	**4.** c	**5.** a
45	**1.** d	**2.** b	**3.** c	**4.** a	**5.** a

46	**1.** b	**2.** d	**3.** a	**4.** b	**5.** c
47	**1.** a	**2.** c	**3.** a	**4.** c	**5.** c
48	**1.** c	**2.** c	**3.** d	**4.** c	**5.** b
49	**1.** d	**2.** a	**3.** a	**4.** d	**5.** c
50	**1.** c	**2.** d	**3.** b	**4.** b	**5.** a

In·Focus 英語閱讀
活用五大關鍵技巧 1

作者	Owain Mckimm / Shara Dupuis / Laura Phelps
譯者	劉嘉珮
審訂	Richard Luhrs
編輯	丁宥暄
企畫編輯	葉俞均
封面設計	林書玉
內頁設計	鄭秀芳／林書玉（中譯解答）
製程管理	洪巧玲
出版者	寂天文化事業股份有限公司
發行人	黃朝萍
電話	02-2365-9739
傳真	02-2365-9835
網址	www.icosmos.com.tw
讀者服務	onlineservice@icosmos.com.tw
出版日期	2024年5月　初版再刷
	（寂天雲隨身聽APP版）160105
郵撥帳號	1998620-0 寂天文化事業股份有限公司

訂書金額未滿1000元，請外加運費100元。
〔若有破損，請寄回更換，謝謝〕

國家圖書館出版品預行編目資料

In Focus英語閱讀：活用五大關鍵技巧（寂天雲隨身聽
APP版）/ Owain Mckimm, Shara Dupuis, Laura
Phelps 著；劉嘉珮譯. -- 初版. --
[臺北市]：寂天文化, 2021.02印刷
冊；　公分
ISBN 978-986-318-966-4(第1冊：16K平裝)

1.英語 2.讀本

805.18　　　　　　　　　　　　　109021539